BOUND TO THE DARK

Claimed by Monsters #1

SADIE MOSS

D1738814

For More Information:
www.SadieMossAuthor.com

Click here to join my mailing list, and I'll send you a FREE copy of
Kissed by Shadows, a prequel novella to my *Magic Awakened* series.

CHAPTER 1

Being fae is not something I would say has a ton of advantages, but there's one obvious benefit to my fae heritage: it makes being a thief a hell of a lot easier.

A grin tilts my lips as I phase through the wall of the massive penthouse apartment I've marked as my target this evening. My body turns incorporeal, and I step easily from the balcony into the living room, as if the thick wall between the two spaces doesn't even exist.

Easy peasy. So far, so good.

The apartment is empty—I'm sure of that, since I watched the owner leave about twenty minutes ago—so I don't worry about being spotted as I glance around the living room. I don't turn invisible when I phase through things, so I had to make sure no one would be home during my attempted theft.

Even though I've taken precautions to make sure I won't be seen or caught, I still have a ski mask on, covering my brunette hair and obscuring my features. The most that anyone who got a look at me could possibly say is that I'm of average height, with a lean build and dark brown eyes, and that could describe thousands of people in this city.

"Okay, Kiara," I mutter to myself. "If you were a super-rich antiquities collector, where would you store your Nightmare Amulet?"

It's sort of a rhetorical question, since I'm about as far from a wealthy antiquities collector as it's possible to be. I'm a twenty-something fae girl who's been masquerading as a human for more than a decade, going to college during the days and using my special abilities to moonlight as a thief at night.

Luckily, I'm a good enough thief that I can still get inside the mind of a rich-as-fuck collector of ancient objects.

If there's a study in this apartment, that's where the object I'm after will be. I got a good look at the guy when he stepped out of the apartment, and he looked uptight and nervous, so I'm sure he keeps all of his most impressive antiquities close at hand in the room where he spends most of his time.

"Study, study, study," I murmur, padding quickly

across the floor as I scan my surroundings. No lights are on, but ambient light from outside allows me to see just fine. It never gets fully dark in New York City. "Where's the damn study?"

As I make my way through the apartment, I phase back in so that I'm corporeal. I can't pick anything up while I'm literally insubstantial, and I'll need to be able to grab the Nightmare Amulet once I find it.

I have no idea why my buyer wants a Nightmare Amulet, but hey, I'm not paid to ask questions, I'm paid to get the job done. And I really, *really* need to get this job done. I need the money.

Once I locate the study, I step inside and begin to search the space. I'm mainly looking for the Nightmare Amulet, but I keep an eye out for an Aurora Gem, just in case.

I check for an Aurora Gem on every job I do, hoping against hope that I'll find one of the incredibly rare supernatural gemstones.

"Fuck," I whisper when my search turns up no sign of a gem. It was a long shot, but I really do need to find one.

Not for any buyer, though.

I need an Aurora Gem for myself.

I stole one from a vampire who's way more powerful and connected than I thought, and now I need to find a replacement, and I need to give it to him before he drains me dry.

Literally.

You can say a lot of things about my life, but calling it boring is not one of them.

My search doesn't turn up a Nightmare Amulet either, but I do find a wall safe hidden behind a painting that looks promising.

As the painting swings away from the wall on silent hinges, I crack my knuckles.

Okay. Time to safe crack.

This is arguably the hardest part of the job. If you're a burglar and you just want to get in and grab whatever art and jewelry you can get your hands on, then excellent, you're in for an easy night. But I've gotten good enough at thievery by now that I have clients asking for specific things—powerful artifacts and rare magical items, the kind of things you just don't keep on display out in the open.

Holding my breath, I pull out my stethoscope, press it to the safe door with one hand, and begin cracking with the other. Fae tend to have particularly good hearing—although our ears are not pointed, thank you very much—which definitely helps. I could drill into the safe, but that would be loud and messy, and the owner would know something had been messed with the second he got home. Plus, I don't want to lug all that equipment around.

After about a minute of fiddling, the safe cracks open. I grin again, mentally patting myself on the back. That was one of my fastest times ever, although it helps that I know what type of model this is and how it works.

Nice work, Kiara.

The safe opens silently on well-oiled hinges, and I tilt my head as I peer inside.

Damn it. There's no Aurora Gem in here either. I swallow hard, trying to shove down my disappointment.

Why the hell did I have to piss off a vampire? As a fae, I couldn't have picked someone worse to get on the wrong side of.

Vampires and fae have a complicated and bloody history. Our blood is like a drug to them, providing them both a rush of pleasure and a boost of power—so for years, they hunted my kind, nearly wiping us out as they drained us one by one. Things have supposedly improved in recent years, but I don't really believe that. I know how fucking terrible vampires can be. I've seen it firsthand. So I don't trust any vampire farther than I can throw them.

Especially not Donovan O'Shae, the vamp I stole the Aurora Gem from. He's very well connected in the supernatural criminal underground of New York, and he's got a reputation for being both ruthless and vicious.

My stomach clenches at that thought. *If he catches me, will he kill me just like the vampires who murdered my parents? Will he drain me dry and tear me limb from limb just because he can?*

Shaking my head to clear it of those awful memories, I refocus my attention on the contents of the safe. It holds a huge stack of money, probably for a rainy day, some velvet boxes that undoubtedly contain jewelry, some documents, what looks like a ledger of some kind, and a small wooden box with a symbol carved on it.

I recognize that symbol. It's a basic warning sigil. It tells you that whatever's inside is potentially dangerous, so be careful. It's not a seal. Seals mean 'don't open this damn thing unless you want to get cursed.' This is more like a 'keep out of reach of children' kind of thing.

Quickly, I pry open the box, and a breath of relief escapes me when I see the amulet nestled inside.

Fantastic.

I double check to make sure there's no camera hidden inside the safe recording me, then hide the box in the pouch I've wrapped around my ribcage. It sits just below my breasts. My boobs are on the large side, and if I wear a push-up bra, then it makes just enough of a shelf that I can hide small objects just underneath and it doesn't distort my shirt. You can't tell there's anything strapped to me.

A *beep* sounds from down the hall, and my head snaps up at the sound.

Shit, that's the alarm turning off. The man who lives here must be home early.

I grimace. At least I've already got the amulet, but now I've got to scramble to get the hell out of here before he catches me stealing from him. He couldn't grab me if I phase out, but this job will get a whole lot more complicated if I'm seen.

I close the safe, then swing the painting back into place to cover it up. With a quick thought, I phase out, turning incorporeal as I hustle out of the office and dart back down the hall.

The owner strides toward the kitchen, tapping something out on his phone as he goes. I take advantage of his momentary distraction and slip past him, practically sprinting down the hall toward the front door.

I reach it before he has a chance to turn around and spot me, slipping right through the door and into the corridor outside.

Ahhh. Sweet freedom.

Now it's time to get paid.

☙❦❧

My fence is a half-goblin named Pat. That's all I know about him, and it's all that I need to know. The relationship between a fence and a thief is one based on trust, but ironically, we need to know as little as possible about each other in order to trust each other.

What if something happened to Pat, and he knew my face, my real name, my home address? He could turn me in. And vice versa. I have to be honest, good fences are hard to find, but I'm not so loyal to Pat that I wouldn't turn him in if it would save my hide. The only person you can rely on is yourself, after all.

So to keep trusting each other, we have to know nothing about each other. I know he gets the goods where they need to go, and I fetch a good price for them, and he knows that I can acquire just about anything a client might want.

Pat's shop is this little pawn place, the kind that has a sign that says "Cash for Gold" and other such tacky posters. There's a mailbox on the wall to the right of the shop door. The shop's got the classic wire grating that comes down at night, but I lift up the mailbox and push aside the fake wall panel to reveal the keypad underneath.

Punching in the code, I look up and down the street, just to make sure I haven't been followed. It's only paranoia if they're not out to get you. And if you're fae, then someone's always out to get you.

Usually vampires.

With the code punched in, the grate opens upward, and the front door unlocks. I slip inside before the timer runs out and the whole thing locks and shuts down again.

The front of the shop where most customers hang out is dark, but there's a light coming from the back room. Pat lives above the shop, or at least I think he does, but this back room is where most of his important dealings go on. It's a messy office, and I'm pretty sure I saw a cockroach in there once, but as long as he gets the job done, it's no matter to me if this place is a dump. After all, I'm not the one living in it.

I keep myself tense and ready to run, just in case. Pat's a fence and generally you leave fences alone. They work for a lot of different clients, they're everybody's friend. But in our world you can never be too careful, and I'm always prepared for the day I slip in and interrupt an unpleasant interrogation.

When I reach the doorway to Pat's office, I see that it's just him, tallying up accounts.

"Heya."

Pat sighs and squints up at me through his glasses. He's smaller than I am, but he could probably kick my ass if he felt like it. He's no slouch. "I wish you'd stop coming here at all hours. My sleep schedule's bad enough already."

"No can do." I pull out the Nightmare Amulet and pass it to him. "Anyway don't clients appreciate a fast delivery?"

The truth was I don't care if clients grumble over waiting an extra twelve hours for their goods. What I care about is not having stolen goods on me for any longer than I need to. I'm never giving the law a chance to catch me or some asshole the chance to set me up. I get the stuff, and I deliver it immediately, no matter what time of day or night it is.

Pat makes a noncommittal humming noise and takes the box from me. I wait patiently as he opens it up and makes sure the thing's authentic. "Mmm. Nice work. He'll be pleased."

I nod. "And do I get paid?"

I always ask for half up front and half when I deliver the goods. Pat takes a cut of the price for connecting me with the client and vice versa. But I won't go into a job without at least some cash as a guarantee. And that way, the client can't cheat me afterwards or pull out.

Pat finishes checking out the amulet and sets it aside. "Yes, yes, you'll get your money."

He gets up and goes over to his other desk, the one that he tends to use just for storage, and crouches down to the bottom of it. I respectfully look away until the desk has swung out of the wall and he's put in the code to open the door to the wall safe and gotten out the money.

That's part of why Pat likes me—I'm polite.

It's clever of him to put his safe down low in the wall. Behind a desk. Most people don't expect that. They expect wall safes to be up high, and if they're behind something, they look for something shallow like a painting or a map hung on the wall.

Pat hands me the cash, and I carefully count it out. That's not impolite, that's just business. If you take the money and go, others will realize that you're new to this business and that they can cheat you. You can trust people, but not too much.

And I don't trust people at all.

The money's the right amount, and I pocket it. "Thanks Pat."

"Stay safe out there."

"You too." Pat's smart and so am I, but you never know when something might go wrong for us. I might show up here someday and Pat's just gone with no word of warning.

I keep my mask on until I leave my fence, and only then do I stop by the spot where I hid my extra clothes with some glamour and change back into my normal outfit, no mask needed.

Changing clothes behind a dumpster in an alley isn't all that glamorous, but not every part of this life is. In fact, most of it isn't, and I got used to making do a long time ago. I have my own apartment now, but I didn't always.

After I lost my parents, I had to live on the streets for a while. I'm not afraid of bad smells.

Once I'm all changed, I put my burglar clothes in my backpack. Now I look just like any other college student out for a night on the town. Glamouring is another fae power that I'm pretty good at. I can make my backpack look like just a pile of bricks by the wall, something nobody will touch while I do my work. If I couldn't do that, it would be a lot harder to stuff my things out of sight until I needed them.

I yank the mask off my face and let out a sigh of relief as I feel the cool air on my skin. I shake out my hair, undoing the tie that's kept it in place. I have thick, long hair, and I've considered cutting it so that it would stay out of the way for burglary work, but I have to admit, I like it too much to chop it off.

Most people trust their fences enough to show their face around them, but I'm not taking any risks. I'm fae. I'm not going to give anyone a chance to sell me out to vampires.

I'm not going to die like my parents did.

Some people claim that things are changing. There's a new king of the vampires here in North America, and they say things are different now. I hear rumors that he's in love with a woman who's part fae, that they're cracking down on vampires feeding off fae, that kind of thing.

But frankly? I'll believe it when I fucking see it.

I'm keeping myself safe. Especially now, with Donovan after me.

My nose wrinkles. I've spent more time thinking about that fucking vampire than I usually do this evening, and it's making me antsy. The idea of going back to my sparse little studio sounds incredibly unappealing. I don't think I could sleep right now, for a lot of reasons.

You know... it's not as late as I thought.

I'm feeling kind of high after a successful burglary job, and I'm flush with cash, which always feels good. Maybe I should stop by Jason's place to say hi.

I nod to myself, making up my mind in a heartbeat and turning left when I step out of the alley. I'm close enough to where Jason lives that I can walk there, so I set off at a fast clip.

Jason is my human boyfriend, and as far as he knows, I'm human too. I've got no intention of telling him otherwise—at least, not for a while. We go to the same college, and I just don't know how to tell him that I'm not what I seem to be. We haven't even been dating seriously for that long, and it feels too risky to reveal my true nature to anyone.

I've been on my own for a long time—almost all my life, ever since the death of my parents—and I just don't know if I'm ready to let someone in like that. I'll have to eventually, if I find a human I want to spend the rest of my life with, even though my eventual goal is to quit thieving. I'm not exactly a fan of the supernatural community, considering how much vampires lord their power over other supernaturals. I'd like to just live like an ordinary human, if that's not too much to ask.

I push those grim thoughts out of my brain as I continue toward Jason's apartment. This isn't the time to think about that shit. I just want to unwind a bit and celebrate another job well done.

Hopefully, he'll still be awake. He's a night owl like

me, so even though it's late, odds are good he hasn't gone to sleep.

Sure enough, when I finally reach his apartment building, I can see a light emanating from his bedroom window. He's probably reading or playing video games in bed.

I let myself in with the key he gave me, stepping silently over a couple pairs of shoes that are piled by the door. Jason's apartment is always a bit messy. It bugs me a bit, but I tell myself to let it go. He's a busy college student, and he's got plenty of other things on his mind. Besides, I came here because I didn't want to face my tiny, almost bare apartment. A little mess is better than that, right?

My apartment is a studio and much smaller than Jason's place. I could use the cash from my work to get myself a nicer place, but I want to save it. College isn't cheap, and I don't know when I might have to cut and run because of my fae heritage. I store all of my cash under a floorboard. Cliché, but it works.

Jason's apartment definitely feels more lived in than mine. Maybe that's part of why I spend more time here than at my own place.

Wanting to surprise him, I close the door quietly behind me. I set my bag down in the entryway and then make my way across the living room, reaching for the hem of my shirt as I go. I figure walking into his room topless will only make the surprise even better.

But just as I start to pull my shirt over my head, I pause when a sound draws my attention. The fabric slips from my fingers as I tilt my head to one side, listening.

Oh my God, is he masturbating?

I can hear him moaning the way he gets during sex, and I snort under my breath. I guess I was wrong about him studying or playing video games. He's clearly found a different way to entertain himself.

Then I hear another noise, higher pitched than the first. A breathy moan filters out from the bedroom, and my eyebrows shoot up to my hairline.

What the fuck?

That second sound definitely wasn't Jason.

It was a woman.

CHAPTER 2

A sick, horrible feeling rises up in my stomach. Even before I storm across the apartment and throw open the bedroom door, I know what I'm going to see.

You know, I think to myself, *shit like this is why I don't trust people.*

I didn't even let Jason in as much as I could have. I told him I wanted to take things kind of slow emotionally, not moving in together yet or anything, and he seemed so understanding about that. I guess now I know why—it's easier to cheat on your girlfriend when she doesn't live with you.

As I throw the bedroom door open, the girl on top of Jason screams and nearly falls off the bed, scrambling to cover up.

"Who are you?" she shrieks.

"Shit," Jason says, which I think rather eloquently sums up the situation.

"Yeah, that sounds about right." I glare at him. "Tell me, Jason, given that I've got a 4.0 GPA, how stupid do you think I am?"

He's well aware that I've got some of the best grades at our school. Work hard, play hard, that's my motto. I'm not going to get anywhere in life without being the best, whether it's at burglary, school, or pretending to be a human. I have every intention of hiding from the supernatural world as much as I can for the rest of my life and that means succeeding in the human world, and humans care about GPAs.

The girl with him looks absolutely mortified. "Are you—? Oh god, I'm so sorry." Now she looks like she might cry. "He told me he was single."

"Well, he sure is single now."

Jason scrambles to his feet. "This isn't what it looks like, babe, come on."

"Oh? Then what does it look like?"

The girl wisely begins grabbing her clothes and starts frantically getting dressed to leave. Yeah, no way I'd stick around for the couple's spat if I was in her position. And frankly, while I'm not mad at her, seeing as she didn't know he was in a relationship, that doesn't mean I want her to be around for this whole fight.

Because this is gonna be a *fight*.

"It's..." I feel like I can see the cogs turning in Jason's brain as he scrambles for some kind of excuse. "You said you wanted to keep things casual!"

"Casual?" *Are you fucking kidding me?* "Right, because 'hey, let's take things a little slow' and 'you're allowed to fuck other people' are completely the same thing! This is not an open relationship!"

The thing that makes me feel extra sick is that if he'd wanted an open relationship, I probably would have said yes. I wanted to take things slow and if he'd wanted to occasionally see other women, that would've been fine with me. But now, I'm just pissed. Because if he's been cheating on me with this girl, what other stuff did he do behind my back?

"You're such a skeezy asshole!" I snap. "How long have you been sneaking other girls into your bed?"

"This is the first time. I swear." His eyes dart guiltily to one side as he says it, and I snort.

"Yeah, right. You're a shitty liar."

"Come on, babe," he pleads, his voice taking on a new tone. "You know you can trust me. This was just one mistake. You know I care about you!" When he sees that his appeals aren't working, he pouts a little. "And besides, how can you talk about not trusting me when I can't even trust you! You don't ever let me in and you don't share anything about your life with me. I don't even know where you live! And you're getting mad at me?"

"You bet your ass I'm getting mad at you." I can't believe he's actually trying to pull this bullshit with me and get me to blame myself for his cheating. "If you had problems in our relationship, you should've talked to me about them, you know, I hear that's something that actual adults like to do."

"Baby, come on—"

Jason reaches for me, but I smack his arm away, then slap him in the face. He reels back, my handprint blooming bright red on his cheek.

"You cheated on me!" I snap. "You fucking—I can't believe this, you little worm. Did you really think I was so stupid that I wouldn't find out? Or that you were so smart you'd be able to keep it from me? Going slow or being casual doesn't equal an open fucking relationship. What the fuck?"

Jason can clearly tell that I'm ready to strangle him, so he wisely doesn't try to say anything more. He sits down on the edge of the bed, and part of me is tempted to keep yelling at him, maybe smack him again, but instead I just start gathering up my things. *It's not worth it,* I tell myself. He's not worth it.

This is why you don't trust anyone. This is why you don't let people in. I didn't even let Jason in as much as I could have. Oh my God, what if I'd told him about my fae nature? What if I'd told him what I really was? An idiot like that cheating on me and knowing that powerful, dangerous information about me? I'd be screwed.

"I'm done," I say shortly, my voice turning hard. "This is over."

"But, babe—"

"Don't." I cut him off. "Don't waste any more empty apologies or excuses on me. And don't call me. We're finished."

With that, I turn on my heel and storm out of the room. Thank fuck I don't have a lot of stuff in his apartment. Tears burn in my eyes as I grab up my things —I don't have a lot here, just some clothes and a toothbrush—trying to ignore Jason, who's followed me out of the bedroom and is watching me.

He's not worth it, I keep telling myself. *He's not worth it. He's not worth it.*

It still hurts.

Ever since my parents died, I haven't let anyone in, but now that I'm in college, I thought... well, I figured maybe it was time to find people to have in my life. And Jason seemed nice and funny. He seemed like a great person to start with. To see what it was like to have someone else in my life besides myself.

Guess I was wrong.

Jason gets some ice for his face as if I punched him instead of just slapped him, glaring at me balefully as I finish stuffing my clothes and other knickknacks into my backpack. I'm lucky there's extra room in the damn thing. I don't think I've been this angry or hurt since I lost my parents.

Not that being cheated on is the same as having your loved ones die. But this is the first time I tried letting someone into my life, and now this is how I'm being rewarded. I feel like throwing up.

"You know," Jason says, his voice accusing, "if you really cared about me, we would be able to talk this out and work through it."

I'm literally on my knees so that I can stuff my shit into my backpack, and I just sigh. The temptation to bury my face in my hands is awful, but I don't want to show any kind of weakness in front of Jason. Not after what he just did. He doesn't deserve to see me vulnerable.

"Or," I reply, "your cheating has shown that you don't really care about me. If you did, you wouldn't have cheated. You wouldn't have gone behind my back."

Honestly, I'm too tired to keep arguing with him. *He's not worth it,* I repeat to myself.

It feels so hollow. Am I not worth it? Am I not worth someone making an effort and being loyal to me? Was that too much to expect? I'm not asking for complete devotion, I'm not asking for someone to hand me the world on a platter. I just want someone to stick to their word and care about how I feel.

"Have a nice life," I tell Jason, getting to my feet and slinging my backpack over my shoulder.

When I get home to my apartment, I immediately feel defeated. I know that's stupid and illogical, but it's true. Coming home with a backpack full of my clothes and random knickknacks to a cold, dark apartment doesn't exactly feel like a victory. Even if I know I'm the one who did the right thing.

Thanks to this stunt I'm going to have to do laundry tomorrow. I just drop my backpack by my laundry basket for now. I could just flop onto the bed and moan, find something to watch, maybe binge one of those cooking competition shows that they do reruns of late at night, eat some ice cream and bemoan my unhappy state.

But why should I let Jason get me so down? Why

should I sit at home crying and let him have all the fun? I know he's not going to waste any time finding someone new. He might protest that he cares about me, but he just showed me what his true colors are. Guys like him don't wait around. They find a new girl immediately.

Well, I can just find myself a new guy.

If my boyfriend isn't going to treat me right, then I'll find someone who will. Not long term. Oh, no. I am fucking *done* with trying to find a real relationship. I should've listened to my instincts, but I just wanted to be fucking normal for once.

Nothing's stopping me from finding a nice one-night stand, though.

I go straight to my closet and open it up, looking for something to wear. There's a dress hanging at the back of my closet that I bought months ago but have never gotten a chance to wear, and I nod in satisfaction as I pull it out and change into it. I tease my dark brown hair a bit and curl it, then put on a touch of makeup around my eyes.

Once I'm all good to go, I head right for a local dive bar. I'm going to have a damn good time, and I'm going to put Jason behind me.

I've actually never been to this dive bar before, although I've walked past it tons of times. There are a few other bars I've frequented, but I haven't been to any since I started dating Jason. We'd just go out to get dinner instead, or we'd hang out at his place.

But now I'm single and fuck it, I want to go to a dive bar. I want to get good and drunk and not think about this. Who knows? If an idiot like Jason can go and get a girl, then I sure as hell can go and get a guy if I want to. I'm sexy, I look like a goddamn Amazon woman, and I know what I'm doing in the bedroom.

The dive bar is actually one of those supernatural bars. Not a lot of humans in here. Whoever I sleep with is going to be supernatural in some way, but hey, that's fine by me. After dealing with Jason, I don't think I want to sleep with a human right now anyway.

The place is dimly lit, the kind of place with posters on the walls from old bands that have played there. Bands with cool names and interesting posters that nobody recognizes because they're a part of that weird underground indie vibe. The floor is sticky and has odd patches of color on it, and I'm pretty sure it was hardwood once upon a time, but at this point, you really don't want to think about it too hard. And you don't want to eat any food that dropped onto the floor.

Over toward the back are a few pool tables and a jukebox. Nobody's touching the latter. A couple of people are around one of the pool tables, halfheartedly playing while talking quietly amongst themselves.

Shifters, by the look of them. They all have the same tattoo marked on their shoulders. Shifters are very loyal to their packs and will often have some sign that shows what pack they belong to. It's not a gang thing, although some humans who see them roaming around might think it is. It's more like if you had your family name tattooed on you.

I get up to the bar and seat myself on one of the stools, raising my hand to the bartender to get a drink. Scanning the few people sitting around, I'm not really seeing a lot of prospects for a one-night stand. It's late, most people have already found someone and left, or they're at a club, or whatever. That's fine. The bartender hands me my martini, and I'm happy to make it the first of many.

So what if I only end up drinking? That'll work just fine. I'll find someone tomorrow when I can actually plan better for it.

A few people scan me up and down. I can sense their gazes, but I ignore them. They don't seem interested in doing more than looking, anyway.

Huh. I guess tonight is a bust.

Resigning myself to just nursing a few stiff drinks and then going home, I polish off my martini and then order another. I'm only halfway through drink number two when the door opens, and three men walk in.

Instinctively, I shoot a glance toward the door to take in the newcomers, and—holy shit.

They're the definition of gorgeous.

They all look to be in their mid-twenties, and there's something so magnetic about them that I swear everyone in the bar just did a double take. The one in front, I'm guessing the leader, has dark brown hair and dark blue eyes, and he's built like a brick house. He's broad all over, shoulders and waist, and I don't think I could fit my hands all the way around his upper arms no matter how hard I tried. My mouth waters. I'm tall, but he could pick me up like I weigh nothing, I'm sure of it.

Behind him, on my right, is a lean guy with dark blond hair and sharp green eyes that practically glow. That alone would tip me off to his supernatural nature if I wasn't already sitting in a supernatural dive bar.

He has a smirk on his face, like he's already anticipating a crazy good time, and I have to admit, it's mesmerizing.

On the left-hand side, looking like the brooding type of boy your mom warns you about, is the third guy. He's also a bit broad, though not as much as the first guy, with blue-black hair and steel-gray eyes. I've never seen anyone who has that hair or that color of eyes. It makes my breath catch in my throat.

He's oddly... beautiful, like he's been carved out of

stone instead of made the way most of us are. What's almost more striking than his hair or eyes are his tattoos that snake up his arms and peek out from his collarbone. They seem to be a series of intricate patterns, like Celtic knots, or the kinds you find decorating mosques. They're gorgeous and must've taken forever to do.

Obviously, these three men are supernatural if they're in this dive bar, but I'm not sure exactly what they are.

They're not vampires, thank fuck, and that's all I care about. Vampires don't go to dive bars like this. They're too fancy for that. At least, in my humble opinion. Then again, I'm biased, but whatever. I've never seen a vampire actually deign to drink with the rest of us, so I'm just speaking from experience.

But I'm not getting any other vibes from them, either.

Hmm. Maybe they're partly human?

That's a thing, especially since a lot of supernatural creatures have a hard time explaining to their human partner what they are until, well, *surprise honey! You're pregnant, and I'm a werewolf!* Being part-human means that the supernatural part of you can be harder to identify specifically since you'll *look* human.

Honestly, doesn't matter. They're hot, and I'm looking to forget about my shitty now-ex boyfriend.

Two of the men head straight for the pool table that's toward the back, and I could weep when I see them bending over with the pool cues. God, they're hot. The third, the leader, heads on up to the bar near me and orders some drinks.

I scan his body up and down, and I make sure that he sees me looking. "I hate to tell you this," I tell him, "but you're a bit too attractive for a bar like this."

The guy snorts, apparently amused, and looks over at me. Fuck, he's even bigger up close. I want to lick my way up his chest. Just looking at him has me hot all over.

"Then what are you doing here?" he asks. As he speaks, I see the tiniest hint of extra-sharp canines. Mmm. That could mean a lot of different supernatural creatures. Most of us have extra-sharp teeth, spoiler alert. The idea of those sinking into my body, leaving bruises, has a shiver running up my spine.

"Maybe I'm waiting for someone to take me out of this place."

The guy's gaze draws slowly up my body, and I shiver again. There's no mistaking the blue fire in his eyes. "I'm North."

"Kiara." I uncross and then re-cross my legs, and his eyes follow the movement. Perfect. If this guy can fuck me against the wall, I'll consider this night a success.

His two buddies seem to have realized that their

friend isn't joining them at the pool table, and they walk over to join us. They're staring at me like I'm their favorite food laid out on a platter. Oh my God.

"Well, well, well," the blond says, smirking at me. "Looks like North made a friend."

"Oh, I'm very friendly," I assure him. Hey, I don't care which of them I go home with. They're all equally sexy.

"I bet you are," the man murmurs. He looks over at North, and they share a pleased look, then turn their attention back to me. "So what are you doing here?"

"She said she's looking for someone to take her away from this place," North says, repeating my words to his friends.

The two other men get these hungry looks on their faces that have my blood rushing. They're not being competitive, or if they are, it's an extremely friendly kind of competitive. Could I be about to nab the luckiest score in the world?

"Her name is Kiara," North adds, speaking to his friends but still looking at me.

"Cain," the blond says. He holds out his hand. I give him my own too, but instead of shaking it, he turns my hand over and kisses the inside my wrist.

If I were standing, my legs would've turned to jelly.

That was possibly the sexiest thing a man's ever done to flirt with me.

"Raven," the third man says, his eyes like chips of steel, his slightly shaggy hair falling a bit into his face.

"Charmed," I reply.

"You look like you've had a bit of a rough night," Cain says. "Drinking alone, rumpled up..."

I shrug and pout. "Well, I just found out my boyfriend was cheating on me, so I broke up with him. Now I'm here, trying to drown my sorrows."

"What kind of idiot would cheat on you?" Raven blurts out, like he can't help himself. The other two look at him, amused.

I can feel my face heating up. "A major idiot," I assure him. "Especially with how... well I took care of him."

All three men look at me like wolves that just sighted a deer. Fuck, yes. I'm not usually great at flirting, but there's no mistaking the heavy aura of tension that hovers around us.

"Well," North drawls, "sounds to me like you should have your revenge."

"And be... taken care of yourself," Cain adds.

"Oh, I'd love that," I promise them. I can barely breathe, but when I finally manage to drag in air through my nose, their scents hit me like a ton of bricks. Each of them smells fucking delicious in his own unique way, all masculine, spicy scents that make my head swim.

Cain glances at North as if asking for permission, and then draws his finger slowly up my thigh. I can't quite hold in my whimper, and the men all grin at each other.

"Wanna dance?" Cain asks, a lopsided grin curving his lips.

"Sure," I breathe, as if I'm worried that speaking too loud will break the spell that seems to be building between us. "With you, or...?"

I glance at the other two men, swallowing. Their whole dynamic is hard to get a read on, but they clearly know each other well and are close. The way they move as a unit, each of them comfortable with and aware of the others, makes me wonder if Cain wants me to dance with just him, or all of them.

He runs a hand through his dark blond hair and grins even wider, his green eyes twinkling. "Well, let's just get out on the dance floor and see what happens, shall we?"

My stomach flips. I nod, taking a quick swig of my drink before sliding off the bar stool. "Okay."

There's a dance floor near the back of the bar, although no one is using it. It's probably only about six feet by six feet, tucked away in the corner so as not to interfere with the serious drinkers who only came here to do one thing. But none of the guys seem bothered about being the only ones dancing as Cain takes my hand and leads me to the floor with the other two right behind us.

One of them must've said something to the bartender before we left the bar—and maybe slipped him a few bucks as well—because as we reach the dance floor, the music coming through the speakers shifts to something with a heavier beat.

"That's more like it." Cain smiles, nodding in approval as he cocks his head to listen for a second.

Stepping closer to me, he wraps an arm around my waist, the thick band of his arm pulling me close as he moves his hips in time with the rhythm.

He's a *really* good dancer. There's something effortless about the way he moves, a natural grace and power, that makes it easy to fall into the same rhythm with him. I let my hips grind against as we move together, and a little thrill runs up my spine when I realize I can feel a bulge down there. He's not exactly sporting a raging erection, but just dancing with me for a few seconds has already gotten a response out of him.

Well, that's an ego boost if there ever was one.

Getting a little greedy and throwing caution to the

wind, I grind against him even more, hitching in a breath when my clit grazes his thigh.

Raven and North are right nearby us, dancing to the song too—but their focus seems to be much more on *me* than on the music. North's gaze runs up and down my body, and I'm sure he notices the way Cain has his leg between my thighs, our hips rolling against each other as we dance.

I'm so distracted by watching North watch us that I don't notice Raven move until he's behind me. A warm, hard body presses against my back, sandwiching me between him and Cain, and my eyes practically roll back in my head when I feel *another* bulge pressing against my ass. He's also getting hard, and it can't even be from touching me, since he wasn't doing that until a second ago.

Is his reaction from watching me dance with his friend?

For some reason, that thought makes my stomach flutter, my pulse picking up in a way that has nothing to do with the exertion of dancing.

Do these men like to watch each other with women? Do they like to do more than watch?

Holy shit.

As if he's read my mind, Cain grabs my hips and spins me around to face his friend, stepping in again to close the distance between us as soon as my back is to him. Now that face I'm looking up at as I dance is Raven's, those steel-gray eyes devouring me as his hands glide down over the curves of my waist.

And then North is there too, his body filling in the space on one side of me. I sway between the three of them, nearly overwhelmed by not just their addictive scents, but by their sheer presence. Any one of these men alone would be a lot of raw masculinity to take in, but all three of them together, so close to me, touching me and gazing down at me?

I feel very much like that deer I imagined earlier.

Except I *want* to be eaten.

I don't know how long we dance for. I'm pretty sure the music changes, but I never pay enough attention to it to really notice when it switches from one track to another.

At one point, Raven goes to the bar to get us all drinks, and even as we down them, we don't stop dancing. I spill a little of my martini on my hand and then laugh as Cain immediately drops his head to lap up the liquid as it trails down my wrist... but the laughter dies in my throat at the feel of his warm tongue on my skin.

My glass disappears from my hand not long after that, and thank fuck it does, because I need my hands free. They're roaming hungrily, moving over each of the men as we continue to dance, shamelessly groping whoever's closest.

The rest of the patrons at the bar are probably staring at us, either amused or annoyed by the foursome of gyrating bodies in corner, but I can't bring myself to worry about that even a tiny bit.

All of the men are sporting bulges in their pants by now, and I can't help teasing them as they pass me back and forth between them. We're still technically dancing, but it's walking right up to the line of "public dry humping."

Finally, North presses in close, his mouth right by my ear. I can feel his warm breath against my skin as he murmurs, "Do you want to get out of here?"

Yes. So badly.

I nod, my core clenching involuntarily as arousal slicks my panties. I can't believe this is happening, but I'll do whatever it takes to make sure it doesn't stop.

He gives a sharp tug on my hand, pulling me closer, and I stumble right against his chest, nearly gasping at the firm muscles I can feel. North lets out a low growl and slides his hand around to press against my lower back, holding me in place as he kisses me.

Oh, fuck.

I've never been kissed like this before. Like someone

is staking a claim, taking something that belongs to him. I feel like I'm melting into a puddle as I cling to his shoulders, whimpering into the kiss.

North pulls back and then turns me toward Cain, who slides a teasing finger under my chin, tilting it up until my throat is exposed. Then he draws his finger slowly down my neck, stopping just above the swell of my breasts. I feel like I'm not even breathing when he kisses me, nipping teasingly at my lower lip.

He pulls away and before I can even react, Raven's kissing me, his tongue sliding between my lips, kissing me deeply, his hands squeezing my hips. It feels like the kind of kiss you see the couple exchange in the rain at the end of the movie, and my knees feel like water.

Raven pulls back, and looks over at North.

North raises his eyebrows at me, as if to say, *what do you think?*

I swallow hard. I've never been so turned on in my life.

"Let's get out of here," I tell him, repeating his previous words.

North smiles, slow and one hundred percent alpha. "Hell, yes."

CHAPTER 3

We head out of the bar, and I can't quite believe this is actually happening. Finding one hot guy is lucky enough but three? And none of them seem jealous of each other. Even among close friends, there can be some competition and jealousy when it comes to finding a hot person to hook up with or date—but all three of them seem to be sharing me.

It just makes them so much hotter.

"I live nearby," I tell them. My apartment's not fancy, but it'll serve. I try to save my money for student loans and things. I don't care if that means I live in a studio.

"Nah." North smirks at me, and more heat runs up my spine. "We've got a great place."

"You'll love it," Cain adds. Immediately it makes me

wonder if that means there are... toys at their place, things they can use on me. I'm so turned on I want to squirm, the heat between my legs starting to feel unbearable.

Surprising for a lot of New Yorkers, they have a car. Raven gets behind the wheel, and I follow Cain into the backseat. North presses up against me from behind, and we pull out.

I've never been so turned on by anyone before. It's like heat is crawling all over me. I feel almost giddy. But hey, I just had a bad breakup, and I did have a martini, and I can't remember the last time I ate, so I'm feeling a little buzzed.

As Raven drives, Cain's hand falls to my thigh again. His fingers stroke my leg, and I have to bite back a whimper.

"You really do want us, don't you?" North asks. He leans in, nosing at my neck. "I can smell the desire in you."

Oh, God, that's so hot. I moan as he starts kissing along my neck. I'm sitting between them on the back seat, my body turned slightly toward Cain and my back pressed against North.

Cain catches my chin between his thumb and fingers as North runs his hand even higher up my leg.

"Yeah, that's it," he encourages. Then he leans in to

kiss me, and I fucking melt. He's a good kisser, so much more skilled than my fuckhead of an ex-boyfriend was. In fact, Jason is the last thing on my mind as Cain's tongue explores my mouth, sinful, seductive, and hungry.

I whimper softly against his lips, and North makes a growling sound from behind me. It sounds almost animalistic, and I can *feel* the vibrations of it where my back is pressed against his broad chest. The sound seems to travel down my body directly to my clit, making it pulse and throb.

My hips shift a little on the seat as I squirm restlessly, trying to subtly clench my thighs together to get a little relief for the ache in my core.

But I should know by now that tonight isn't about being subtle. I picked up three of the hottest guys I've ever seen in my life in a bar, I'm about to hook up with all three of them... and we all know it.

Subtlety is so far in the rearview mirror that I can't even see it anymore.

As if to prove my point, North grips my thigh with one large hand, spreading my legs wider instead of letting me press them together. Then his lightly calloused fingertips trail upward, grazing the skin of my thigh in a way that makes me shiver.

"You're wet," he murmurs roughly as his fingers brush over the damp fabric of my panties.

Fuck, I know I am. I can feel my arousal soaking into the fabric, hot and damp. I have a second to wish that I'd worn sexier panties for this occasion, but then the thought is driven from my mind as North tugs the crotch of my panties to one side and drags a thick finger through my soaked folds.

"Fuck," I mutter into Cain's mouth, and I swear I can feel the gorgeous, charming man smile against my lips.

He breaks our kiss to draw back and gaze at me with heated green eyes, as if he wants to see the effect his friend is having on me.

"She likes that," he tells North, leaning in to nip at my lower lip. "Should we make her come right now? Right here? Give her a little taste of what she's in for?"

"Hell, yes."

North's voice is gruff and deep, and as he speaks, he drives two fingers into me. I hiss out a breath and arch my hips, leaning more of my weight against him as sensation rushes through me. I'm wet enough that there's no resistance, and my body stretches around his fingers as he starts to fuck me with them, grinding the heel of his hand against my clit.

Cain rests his hands on my knees, tugging my legs

even wider apart. I can feel cool air against the heated flesh of my pussy and inner thighs, and the idea that I'm so exposed for these men only cranks my arousal up even higher.

When Cain drops his head to suck lightly at the skin of my neck, I glance up toward the front of the car, where Raven is driving. His gaze flicks upward to watch us in the rearview, and our eyes meet.

God, he's so beautiful.

Even now, his face hardly has any expression, his chiseled features blank and stoic. But his gray eyes burn with a heat so intense that it reminds me of molten metal, and his nostrils flare slightly as he drags in a sharp breath.

He's getting turned on by this, I realize. By listening to his friends drive me crazy in the back seat. By stealing glances of us as he deftly navigates us down the streets of New York.

I lose sight of Raven as North begins to fuck me even harder with his fingers, making my eyes roll back in my head. I'm about to detonate like a fucking bomb, and we haven't even gotten back to their place yet.

As if he can read my body like a damn book, North murmurs, "You're gonna come, aren't you? Let go for me, beautiful. I want to be the first one to make you come."

There's something about the possessive tone of his

voice, especially when I know he's watching his friend suck a hickey onto my neck, that makes heat burst through me. They're clearly willing to share, but it's like they each want a piece of me just for themselves too.

I like that.

I don't really know why I like it as much as I do, but it makes me moan softly, my eyelids fluttering as I writhe between the two gorgeous men.

And when North drops his head and bites my earlobe, I do exactly what he commanded.

I come.

Hard.

My hips buck up against his touch, forcing his fingers deeper inside me as I grind wildly against the heel of his hand.

"Oh, shit! Oh, fuck! I'm coming... I'm..."

My words trail off on a cry. One of my hands reaches behind me to palm the back of North's neck while the other fists the front of Cain's shirt, dragging his mouth up to mine for a sloppy, desperate kiss.

He fucks my mouth with his tongue, mirroring the way North is thrusting his fingers into me as I ride out my orgasm, and when I finally slump between the two of them, he draws back.

His perfectly shaped lips curve up into a devastatingly sexy smile. It's charming and a little smug, and the sight of it makes my pussy clench around North's fingers.

"You make the prettiest sounds when you come," he tells me, his eyes gleaming wickedly. "You smell fucking incredible too. I wonder if you taste as good as you smell."

I barely have time to register the fact that the smell of my arousal has completely filled the car before Cain nods to North in some silent signal.

"I've got her," North murmurs from behind me. He drags his fingers out of my pussy and wraps one arm around me, pulling me tighter against him as he adjusts our position on the seat, turning us until we're almost completely facing Cain.

When he grips my chin just like his friend did earlier, I can feel the wetness on his fingers, and it sends a dirty little thrill through me.

"Watch Cain, Kiara," North tells me roughly. "Look how hungry he is for you."

I swallow hard, my heart fluttering like a hummingbird as I stare at the gorgeous blond man. His tongue darts out to lick his lips, and I swear I almost come again on the spot just from the sight of it. His green eyes meet mine for a second before his gaze drops down to where my legs are spread, my pussy barely covered by my panties. Then he scoots back farther on the seat, giving himself enough room to lean down and bury his face between my legs.

"Oh, shit," I squeak, grabbing a fistful of North's hair and arching against him as the wet warmth of Cain's tongue slides over my already throbbing clit.

My body feels like it's on fire, like I'm so hot that I might spontaneously combust, and even though little aftershocks of pleasure from my first climax are still rippling through me, I can feel another orgasm gathering deep in my core.

I've come multiple times on plenty of occasions, but that was all thanks to my trusty vibrator.

I've *never* come more than once during sex.

Hell, the last time I had multiples was after a particularly disappointing round of sex with Jason. He didn't even get me over the finish line before he hit his own climax, and then he promptly passed out. So I took my favorite romance novel and my B.O.B. into the other room and had a one woman party that made me see stars.

Tonight, though?

These men are about to put me on the 'multiple O' train, and none of them have even been inside me yet.

That thought makes a surge of heated anticipation rush through me as I imagine what's still to come. Any last inhibitions I might've had about doing this fall away as I thread the fingers of my free hand into Cain's silky blond hair and grip the strands tightly, grinding against his face to chase my pleasure.

I'm probably close to suffocating the poor guy, but he doesn't seem to mind one bit. His tongue works faster, slipping and sliding all over my clit before he stiffens it and drives it into my pussy the same way I hope like hell he'll do later with his cock.

"Make her scream again," Raven says hoarsely from the front seat, and I realize he's still watching us. I can hear the strain in his voice, just like I can feel the heat of North's cock against my lower back where he's got me held between his legs.

They're all getting turned on by this, and I haven't really even touched them properly yet. They *like* this. They each like watching and listening to what the others do to me.

Maybe that's why I decide to give Raven exactly what he wants.

When Cain returns his attention to my clit, flicking his tongue over the sensitive bud in rapid movements, I let my eyes fall shut as my mouth opens on a keening cry.

I'm thrashing between North and Cain, held in place by Cain's strong hands and North's firm body, barely aware of anything except the pure lightning bolt of pleasure that shoots through me as I come again.

Cain doesn't let up either. He pushes me right to the edge of what I can take, continuing to lap at me as my clit turns even more sensitive in the aftermath of my second orgasm. When I give a sharp tug on his hair, he finally relents, lifting his head and grinning up at me as he licks his lips again.

His full lips are shiny with my arousal, and my stomach clenches at the way he trails his tongue over them like he's still starving for the taste of me.

Holy shit. How the fuck did my night end up like this? Somehow, it went from being one of the worst evenings of my life to something I'm sure I'll think about until my dying day.

"What does she taste like?" Raven rasps from the driver's seat, and Cain glances up toward him as North reaches up to cup my breasts, rolling my nipples between his fingers through the fabric of my clothing.

"Like fucking heaven," Cain reports, grinning slyly at me while he speaks. "Like the sweetest kind of honey."

The car lurches as Raven speeds up, whipping around a Mercedes in front of us so fast that Cain, North, and I all slide sideways a little on the back seat.

Cain throws his head back and laughs at his friend's response, and I can't help but grin too.

I only met these men a short time ago, but their easy camaraderie makes me feel like I've known them longer than I actually have. A giddy, happy feeling rushes through me, and I twist a little in North's embrace so that I can find Raven's eyes in the rearview mirror.

"Are we there yet?" I ask, dragging my lower lip through my teeth.

His nostrils flare, and he jerks the wheel again, cutting down a narrow side street where there are no cars in our way.

Cain and North both laugh, and North keeps teasing my breasts while Cain leans in to kiss me again. I can taste myself on his tongue, and it really does taste like fucking heaven.

Before we can lose ourselves in it too much, the car slides to a stop. The purr of the engine cuts out, and Cain pulls back, arching a brow at me as his lips curve up on one side.

"I think Raven wants a turn," he murmurs sinfully.

He slides back and opens the door, helping me out of the car as North releases me from his hold. North gets out on the other side—or at least, I think he does. I don't really get a chance to see, because as soon as my feet are on the ground, Raven appears in front of me. His expression is unreadable, but it's hard to misinterpret the blazing heat in his eyes.

His large, calloused hands frame my face, and for just a second, time seems to slow. We're suspended in that moment of breathless anticipation for a single heartbeat.

Then his lips crash down on mine.

CHAPTER 4

Raven kisses the way he seems to do pretty much *everything*—silently and with single-minded focus.

His hands delve into my hair, angling my head up as he stands so close to me that our chests brush. He's so tall that he has to drop his head a lot to make our lips meet, and even then, I'm nearly standing on my tiptoes. Something about the way he looms over me makes me feel tiny and fragile, and although those are feelings I normally hate, a gush of wetness dampens my panties.

I cling to his forearms, then reach up and wrap my arms around his neck, dragging him down even lower as I mold my body against his.

"Sweet," he mutters, as if he's confirming to himself

that everything Cain told him in the car about the way I taste is true.

His voice is gruff, deeper than I've ever heard before —the few times he's spoken, anyway—and he makes a sort of rumbling sound in his throat as he takes a few steps, walking me backward and pressing me up against the side of the car.

The passenger door got shut at some point when I wasn't paying attention, and the metal is cold against my heated skin, even through the fabric of the dress. I hiss out a breath, and Raven takes the opportunity to kiss me even deeper, plunging his tongue into my mouth and sucking on mine like he's trying to steal a piece of my soul while he's at it.

"Please... oh, shit. Fuck... I want..."

I'm babbling. There's no other word for it.

Every word comes out muffled and breathless in between heated kisses, and I can't seem to form a complete sentence to save my life. I'm aware of Cain and North watching the two of us, and even though neither of them are touching me at the moment, their intense gazes are affecting my body the same way Raven's stare did in the car.

I've never even done a three-some, let alone a four-some, but I had no idea how much it would turn me on knowing that I'm being watched. It's not an exhibitionist kink, exactly. I sure as fuck hope no one is walking by on the street right now and getting a glimpse of whatever this looks like.

I don't want just *anyone* watching me.

Only Cain and North.

I want them to see how turned on they made me, to know that they lit the fire that's consuming Raven and me right now.

Raven's fingers leave my hair, and he takes advantage of the fact that I'm pressed up against the car, using the opportunity to run his hands over every inch of me. When he gets down to my ass, he grabs a handful of it, digging his fingers into the flesh of my butt so hard that I whimper.

I hook my leg around his muscular waist at the same moment he lifts me, and a full body shudder works its way through me as the hardness of his cock grinds against my swollen, needy clit.

It's too much.

Too fucking good, on top of everything else.

I'm about to come again, right here on the street.

And hell, maybe I do have a little bit of an exhibitionist streak, because I don't even try to stop it. I just wrench my lips away from Raven's and bury my face in his neck, holding on for dear life and wrapping my other leg around his waist too as pleasure shoots through my body like a runaway rocket.

He groans, and I swear I can feel the hard, heavy thickness of him pulse against me as he shifts his hips in a circular pattern, dry humping me to ride me through my orgasm.

"Oh, holy..." I pant against his neck, breathing in the earthy, smoky scent that clings to his skin. "Fuck."

"Yeah, that's sounding pretty damn appealing right about now," Cain comments, his voice hitting my ears like the sexiest kind of music. "Should we get inside, or did you actually plan to fuck her out here, Raven?"

"Don't care," the man holding me grunts, still grinding his hips against mine as my toes curl in my shoes.

Part of me thinks he's just talking dirty, caught up in the wild, hedonistic insanity of this night. But another part of me isn't entirely sure he wouldn't tear my dress off, shove his pants down, and plunge into me right here on the side of a quiet New York street.

My pussy clenches at the thought, almost like it's begging for him to do just that, but I shake my head quickly, clinging to the last few shreds of good sense I have left.

"Inside," I pant. "Now."

Cain chuckles, and North makes a soft growling

sound as Raven hauls me away from the car. He doesn't put me down, just turns away from the sleek vehicle and starts striding toward the building they've brought me to, his steps heavy and purposeful.

Normally, I'm not the kind of girl who likes to be carried around, but tonight seems to be about breaking all of my "normals," so I don't resist or try to squirm out of his hold. I just stay wrapped around him like a vine, dropping hungry kisses to the exposed skin of his neck.

He has even more tattoos than I realized a first. There are a lot of them, it seems, the dark ink peeking out above the collar of his shirt almost all the way around his neck. I have a feeling they cover almost his entire torso and back, judging by how much of his neck is tatted up, and I suddenly can't wait to get inside so I can tear off his shirt and get a good look at him.

At all of them, really.

A door opens, and I'm jostled slightly as Raven carries me up the stairs that lead to their walk-up. I drag my lips and teeth over his neck, feeling almost drugged with lust and trying to take this opportunity to get my equilibrium back before we get to their apartment and clothes start flying.

I knew back at the bar that I was in for a wild night. I mean, fuck, I basically threw myself at three guys who are obviously close, letting the sexual tension between us swell until I agreed to go home with them. There was no question about what we all wanted when we piled into the car to head back to their place.

But now that we're here, I can feel butterflies flapping around wildly in my stomach.

This is really happening.

Not just several intense make-out sessions in a car. Not just grinding against a guy until his friends watch me come. A whole hell of a lot more than either of those things.

I'm going to fuck all three of them.

The thought passes through my mind, and I feel like a damn nymphomaniac..., but I can't deny it's what I want. I want all of them, and since this is a night I'm sure I'll never get to repeat, I can't find any reason not to take what I want.

"Fuck, I wish we lived on the first floor," Cain mutters, and I giggle against Raven's warm skin.

A moment later, we step off the stairs and head down a short hallway. North unlocks the door to their apartment, and all three men stride inside. The moment the door closes behind us, I feel two hot, hard bodies step in on either side of me, enclosing me completely between the three friends.

Raven unwinds my legs from around his waist, setting me back on my feet as several pairs of lips brush over my skin, sending goosebumps scattering across my flesh in all directions. For a moment, I'm paralyzed by the overwhelming amount of sensation—I don't know where to turn first, who to arch closer to, or who to kiss.

As if sensing my physical and emotional overload, North nips at my ear then catches my chin with his fingertips, turning my head so that our eyes can meet.

"Have you ever done this before, beautiful?" he asks, his voice husky. "Been with three men at once?"

"No."

I shake my head, the word falling from my lips on a husky whisper. Maybe I should lie and say I have, just so I don't seem like I'm completely out of my depth here. But I'm a horrible liar, and I don't think they'd believe me anyway.

"Good." A smile spreads across his lips, more possessive than any expression I ever saw Jason wear. "We'll take care of you. I promise."

"Have you done this before?" I blurt, my eyes practically rolling back as Cain drags the tip of his tongue up my neck. "Shared a woman."

"No." Something burns in North's dark blue eyes, and he shakes his head once. "Never. You'll be our first."

I'm a little shocked by his answer. I almost regretted the question as soon as I asked, because I didn't want to open the door to hearing about a bunch of their sexual exploits with other women.

But the fact that they've never shared is a little mind-boggling, especially when they're all gorgeous as models and are clearly very close. I can't imagine a lot of women would tell them no if these three gorgeous specimens offered them a night of no-strings-attached sex.

A little flicker of pride runs through me, an echo of the possessive look I saw on North's face a moment ago. Not that long ago, we were all strangers in a bar. But even though we barely know each other, this night is special. It's something out of the ordinary for all of us. A first for all of us.

And that means something.

"I don't... I don't really know how it's supposed to go," I admit, my face heating up a little. "Do you...? Should I...?"

I trail off, my cheeks so warm by this point that I'm sure they're bright red. I've had sex enough times that I'm definitely familiar with where everything goes, but that was when there were only two people involved. With three men and only one me, I'm not sure what the protocol is here.

"You're doing great so far, babe," Cain tells me with a crooked grin, a note of heated approval in his voice.

"And there is no 'supposed to.' Just do what feels good. We want you to enjoy this."

Fuck, I'm already enjoying this so much that my panties are a soaking wet mess. But I like that he said that. It eases my nerves a little, giving me the confidence to wrap my arms around Raven's neck and kiss him again, grinding against the hardness that presses into my lower belly.

He plunges his tongue into my mouth, giving me another taste of his unique, addictive flavor. Then he pulls away and drops to his knees in front of me, sliding his hands down the sides of my body and lingering on every curve like he's trying to memorize them.

Holy shit. He's going to—

I don't even have the time to properly form the thought before he reaches up beneath the hem of my dress and hooks his fingers into the waistband of my underwear, dragging them down my legs in one quick, smooth movement. Letting them drop to the floor around my feet, he shoves my skirt up and buries his face between my legs.

"Fu—"

All the breath is punched from my lungs by the rush of sensation as he starts to eat me out with wild abandon. He's the second one of these men to have his mouth on me tonight, and the contrast between him and

Cain is as clear as day in the way they each go down on a girl.

Cain was all sensual teasing and passionate hunger.

Raven is like an unleashed hurricane, like raw power distilled down to its purest form.

He grabs my hips tightly as my legs turn into wobbly noodles, holding me upright as he continues to devour me. I reach down to rest one hand on the top of his head, sliding my fingers through his thick blue-black hair as I fight to keep my balance. Cain and North step back a little to watch their friend eat me out, and I let out a helpless whimper as I watch them both pull off their shirts.

They're fucking gorgeous.

Neither of them are tattooed like Raven is, but their bodies are sculpted and hard, with broad chests and washboard abs that look entirely too lickable.

When they reach down to unzip their pants, my breath catches in my throat.

Moving almost at the same time, they each shove their pants down enough to draw out their cocks, and I swear I can feel drool pooling in the corner of my mouth.

Shit, that's hot.

They're both big, and my gaze bounces between the two of them as they start to stroke themselves. North rolls his thumb over the broad head of his cock, gathering the precum spilling from the tip to spread it over the length of his shaft as he works his fist up and down. Cain works himself in short, fast strokes, his eyes burning with fierce lust as he does.

Just as I'm on the verge of being hypnotized by the sight of these two stunning men jerking themselves off, Raven scrapes his teeth softly over my clit, making me jerk against him.

He doesn't speak, but he looks up at me through his lashes as I glance down at him, and the sight of him on his knees before me, coupled with the sounds of the two other men stroking themselves, is almost enough to have me hurtling over the edge once again.

But Raven doesn't let me come. He drags his tongue slowly all the way from the bottom of my pussy to the top, lapping up my arousal, then leans back and stands up. A second later, he picks me up again. Except this time, instead of wrapping his arms around me, he throws me over his shoulder.

I let out a surprised sound as all the blood rushes to my head—partly because of gravity and partly because I know my dress is riding up high enough that my ass and pussy are on full display.

"Which bedroom?" Raven asks, his voice rumbling in his chest.

"Well, we all know yours is a mess," Cain jokes.

Then he chuckles. "I guess mine is too. So, North's it is then."

Raven starts walking down the hall, and it occurs to me that I have no real idea what this place looks like. I didn't really take the time to check it out when we entered, since I was a little distracted by the feeling of three men worshipping my body.

When we enter a new room, I get a quick glimpse of an immaculately organized space before Raven tosses me down onto a large bed. I bounce a little as I land on the mattress, and all three men come to stand at the foot of the bed, gazing down at me.

I twist my legs a little, desperate for friction, arousal shooting through me at the way they're looking at me. My panties are gone entirely by now, abandoned in the entryway when Raven picked me up, and my dress is bunched up around my waist, leaving my lower half on full display.

"Take off your dress," North commands, his gaze trailing hungrily over my body.

I've never had a guy boss me around in bed. Well, that's not entirely true. Jason tried once, but I kept getting the giggles because he put on this weirdly fake deep voice to do it.

But there's nothing weird or fake about the growly, dominant tone in North's voice as he tells me to lose the dress, and it's almost like my body starts obeying the command before my mind consciously tells my limbs what to do.

Grabbing the fabric of my dress with both hands, I arch my back and sit up partway to tug it off, then toss it on the floor as I settle back onto the bed.

"Now you," I say, and the husky rasp in my voice definitely isn't fake either.

North grins. I get the feeling he's not the kind of guy who takes orders from many people, but he and the others don't miss a beat as they quickly strip.

I can't keep my eyes off them as they shed their clothes, my gaze drifting back and forth between the three of them as I try to absorb everything all at once. There's so much raw masculinity on display that some part of my brain thinks this can't possibly be real.

Maybe I'm still back at the bar right now, slumped over in a corner booth somewhere having a wet dream after too many martinis.

Well, whatever. Even if this is just a dream, it's the best fucking dream I've ever had. And I'm going to make the most of it.

My lower lip is trapped between my teeth, and I bite down harder as I stare at the tattoos covering Raven's skin. They're all done in black ink, detailed and ornate, and I would probably spend hours studying them if not

BOUND TO THE DARK

for the fact that there are two other gorgeous men drawing my attention.

North is muscled and solid, with a dusting of hair across his chest and abs so cut I want to sit up and lick them. Cain is lean and gorgeous, with tan skin, a narrow waist, and a fucking gigantic cock.

He grins when he catches me staring at it, and I know I'm blushing when my cheeks heat up.

Still smiling with cocky, hungry self-assurance, he glances over at North. "Condoms?"

"Nightstand."

Cain winks at me, then strolls over to a nightstand next to the bed and opens a draw near the top. He reaches in and pulls out three foil-wrapped condoms, and my breath catches in my throat.

This is it. I'm really going to do this.

I'm about to fuck all three of these men.

CHAPTER 5

The look on my face must tell the guys exactly what I'm thinking, because Cain's eyes darken a little as he steps closer to the bed.

"Do you want us, Kiara?" he asks, although the tone of his voice makes it pretty clear he knows the answer already. "You want me and my brothers to fuck you?"

As he speaks, he tosses two of the condoms down on the bed, reaching down with his free hand to grip his dick. He strokes his shaft slowly, almost like he's teasing both me and himself by dragging his fist up and down his length.

More arousal trickles from my pussy, smearing over my thighs, and I lick my lips as I nod.

"Yes," I rasp.

"Good. Because we all want you."

He grins down at me, making dimples pop out on his cheeks, then hands me the condom. I blink at it for a second, then scramble up onto my knees and snatch it out of his hand. My heart is pounding so hard and fast that it's making blood rush in my ears, and my hand shakes a little as I unwrap the condom.

Cain's hand closes over mine, and I look up at him.

"Don't worry," he says, and although that teasing heat is still in his tone, I can hear sincerity too. "We'll take care of you. We'll make you feel so good you'll be ruined for all other men. We'll make you come so many times that you'll be hoarse from screaming our names. I promise."

I nod, and he grips his cock at the base as I start to slide the condom on. He releases it as I roll the condom down over his shaft, hissing out a breath as his head tips backward.

"Fucking hell," he groans, shooting a glance at the other two men as he chuckles. "If she feels so good just doing *this*, I can't wait to be inside her."

They both make appreciative noises, and a rush of confidence swells inside me. As soon as the condom is on, I grab the back of Cain's neck and pull him down into a messy kiss, falling back onto the bed and bringing him with me.

He crawls up over me, settling his hips between my

thighs. The hot, thick length of his cock slides through my folds as he rolls his hips against mine, and I whimper into his mouth.

Something seems to shift in him at that, and a little of the teasing, charming Lothario vanishes. He breaks our kiss, hooking his hands under my knees to drag me a little closer to him as he finds my entrance with his cock.

I wasn't wrong earlier. He's big.

Fucking *huge*.

I tense a little, my back arching automatically. "Shit, you're too big."

"Not for you, baby," he murmurs, pressing deeper with small pumps of his hips. "You can take me. I know you can."

Shit. Shit. Shit.

Shiiiiiit.

As he works his way deeper inside, opening me up, his thumb finds my clit. My eyes practically roll back into my head, and he slides in another few inches as I moan and gasp beneath him.

"Does that feel good?" he demands, his gaze riveted on my face.

"Yes." I nod wildly, worried that if I don't answer right away, he'll stop. And fuck, I don't want him to stop. "It feels so good. So good. So. *Big.*"

"For fuck's sake. His ego's already big enough,"

someone mutters next to us, and I glance over quickly to see Raven rolling his eyes.

I would laugh if I had the breath to do it, but all the air is punched from my lungs as Cain finally bottoms out inside me. He drops his head to kiss me, and I wrap my legs around his waist and my arms around his shoulders, clinging to him like a baby monkey as my clit throbs.

"Look at my brothers," Cain murmurs as our kiss breaks. "Do you see them watching me fuck you? Can you see what it's doing to them? They're wishing they were inside you right now, just like I am. They're imagining how good you'll feel. Fucking perfect."

As his dirty words fill my ears, he starts to thrust, going a bit slow at first to give me time to acclimate to his size. But he doesn't wait long before he starts to pick up speed, and the bed rocks a little beneath us as our bodies start to move in sync.

It's hard to keep my eyes open or focus on anything but the barrage of sensations coursing through me, but I do what Cain ordered and turn my head to gaze at his brothers. Raven is stroking his cock as he watches us, swirling his fist over the crown to gather the beads of precum that seep from the little slit at the tip, and North's jaw is clenched tight, fire burning in his blue eyes.

"Oh, *fuck*," I moan, tightening my grip around Cain's shoulders.

I'm about to come again, and I'm pretty sure he is too.

But then he stops.

"What—?"

I jerk my attention back to him, my jaw falling open. He grins, pressing deeper inside me once more and grinding hard so that the base of his cock rubs right against my clit.

"I told you we'd take care of you, babe," he murmurs. "Trust me."

With that, he pulls all the way out, kneeling between my legs. Before I can work up the words to protest, he draws me up so that I'm on my knees on the mattress too. A warm body fills the space behind me, and I realize that Raven has crawled up to join us.

"Open up for me," Cain murmurs, lifting me off the mattress so I can wrap my legs around him again. He slides inside me once more, and even though there's still a stretch, my body welcomes him easily this time.

Raven moves in closer behind us, and I shiver when I feel his hard cock nestle between my ass cheeks.

Oh my god, is he going to fuck me there? While his friend is still inside me?

A flicker of worry makes my stomach flutter as I

think about taking him in my ass, but it's followed by a thrill of excitement. I don't know if my body could handle that, but there's a part of me that sure as hell wants to try.

Rather than working his way into my back hole, though, Raven slides his cock between my ass cheeks, using me to get himself off. He matches his tempo to Cain's, and with my body pinned between theirs, there's nothing I can do but hang on for the ride and let myself feel everything they're doing to me.

The mattress shifts a little, and when I realize that North has joined us on the bed, I grope for him blindly. His calloused fingers wrap around my hand, bringing it to his cock, and he hisses out a breath as I start to stroke him.

I lose track of time as all of them encase me between them on the bed, each of us moaning and panting.

Then Raven grunts behind me, dropping his head to bite the spot where my neck meets my shoulders.

"Come for us," he growls. "Come again. Now."

A second after he finishes speaking, fingers find my clit. I honestly don't know whose they are at this point, but it hardly matters when the orgasm that's been hanging out in the wings rushes over me, making me thrash between them.

"Fuck," Cain grunts. "You're making it hard to hold on, baby."

"Let me have a turn before you blow your load like a teenager," Raven says.

He sucks on my neck to punctuate his words, and Cain chuckles. He pulls out of me, and I lose my grip on North's cock as he sets me down on my knees on the bed. Cain backs up a little, and he and North watch as Raven puts a hand on my upper back, urging me to bend over.

I do, feeling filthy and sexy at the same time as I drop down onto all fours on the bed. I can hear him rolling on a condom, and then his large hands grip my hips as he sinks into me.

"Holy fuck," I whimper.

He's almost as big as Cain, and my already overloaded nerve endings are having a fucking field day as my body tries to process all the sensations at once.

Raven's fingers find my clit again, and he works them in gentle circles as he starts to slide in and out of my soaked core. In front of me, Cain gazes down at me with a heated expression before reaching down to tug off the condom.

"I thought I wanted to come inside that sweet pussy," he murmurs roughly. "But watching you get fucked by Raven like that? It makes me want to be inside you again. Your mouth, this time. You good with that?"

It takes me a second to answer. His words, along with the feel of Raven driving into me at a steady pace, sets me off again, and I bow my head as another orgasm roars through me. When I finally look up, I'm sure my hair is disheveled and my eyes are a little glazed.

"Yes," I whisper. "Please."

A broad, sexy as fuck grin spreads across Cain's face in response.

"So fucking perfect," he repeats, moving closer to give me what I want.

My lips wrap around his cock at the exact moment Raven slams into me harder from behind, and the force of it makes my mouth slide down over Cain's shaft. All three of us groan.

"That's right. Just like that." His fingers tangle in my hair as Raven starts to fuck me harder. "I can feel how turned on you are."

I'm not surprised. It's like my entire body is buzzing with it, as if I've transcended the physical plane and entered some sort of dimension where nothing exists but pleasure. I hollow my cheeks and suck harder as I drag my tongue over the underside of Cain's cock, and the sound of Raven's hips slapping against my ass fills the room.

"Yes. Yes. Fucking *yes*."

Cain's face contorts with pleasure, and he works his hips in short, choppy thrusts, fucking my mouth just like Raven is fucking my pussy from behind. Then his jaw drops open, his hand tightening on my hair. A second later, the first salty splash of his cum hits my tongue.

I groan around him, licking and sucking as he explodes in my mouth.

"Shit, that's hot," Raven hisses, driving into me once more and then going still as his cock throbs inside me. I clench around him, and he groans as he pulses again, filling up the condom with his release.

For a second, we stay just like that, all three of us connected with me in the middle. Then Cain slowly draws out of my mouth. I suck in a breath, realizing belatedly that I've gotten a little low on oxygen.

He pushes my hair out of my face, tucking a lock behind my ear as he leans down to kiss me.

"I love the taste of my cum on your lips," he whispers, and I moan softly.

The fucking mouth on this guy. His dirty talk alone could wreck me.

Raven bends over to pepper kisses along my shoulders, burying his face in my hair and inhaling deeply before he finally pulls out of me.

I feel strangely empty all of a sudden, and my limbs

are shaky from exertion and an overload of pleasure. Deciding not to fight it, I collapse onto the mattress, staring up at all three men with a goofy smile on my face.

"See?" Cain grins down at me. "I told you we'd make it good for you."

"You wore her out," North rumbles in his deep voice.

I glance over at him, my gaze locking with his. There's heat and pride in his expression, as if he really enjoys the sight of me sprawled out on the bed and thoroughly fucked by the two men he calls his brothers. He's still hard as a rock, his cock jutting out from his body, and the sight of it makes something stir inside me.

He's not wrong.

I'm definitely worn out. I've never, *ever* been fucked like that. I've never come so many times in a row, especially not the kinds of orgasms that seem to fill my body to the brim with pleasure.

But I'm not done.

Because I haven't felt what it's like to have North inside me yet.

And for some reason, I feel like I'll die if I don't.

"Come here," I whisper, holding out a hand to him. I feel strangely shy as I wait for him to respond, as if worried that he'll say no or something.

But he doesn't.

He moves closer, bracing one hand on the mattress

as he leans down to kiss me. He tastes like whiskey, and he smells like cedar and woodsmoke, and I can't help reaching up to bury my fingers in his dark brown hair.

Without breaking our kiss, I shift my position on the bed, rising up onto my knees. When I finally tear my lips away from his, it's only so that I can drag them down his neck, over his chest, and along the washboard ridges of his abs.

Then, just like I did with Cain, I wrap my lips around the broad head of his cock.

"She's fucking good at that, isn't she?" Cain comments as North tips his head back, the muscles of his neck straining.

Maybe the regular version of me would be embarrassed by his comment. Maybe the me who hadn't thrown herself headfirst into a foursome with three gorgeous men would be shocked by the idea of going down on two men one after the other.

But wherever that version of me is, she definitely wasn't invited to this party.

I moan around North's cock as sparks of arousal prickle under my skin, bobbing my head faster. He curses under his breath, and I wrap one hand around him, sliding it up and down along with my lips.

"She's hungry as fuck for him," Raven comments.

I don't respond to his words since my mouth is a

little busy right now, but I glance sideways at him as I keep working North's cock. He's hard again, and the sight of his cock standing at attention as he watches me blow his brother makes me squeeze my thighs together, my body desperate for friction.

My mouth moves faster, and I can't stop my hips from following that example. I'm practically humping the air, my body desperate for something I can't even quite name. It feels like more than desire, like a hunger that will never be fully satisfied.

"You're close again, aren't you?"

North's gruff voice pulls me out of my thoughts. I swallow, nodding a little as I tilt my head to look up at him.

"Do you want more?" he asks.

I nod again, so enthusiastically that his cock slips out of my mouth. He smiles just slightly, the curve of his lips cracking his stoic expression. For some reason, I'm not at all embarrassed that he knows how much I want him. Maybe it's because I know this is only going to be a one-night stand, so I don't feel any need to hold things back or try to play it cool. We only have a limited time together, so I need to take advantage of every second.

Keeping his gaze on me, North picks up the last condom sitting on the bed and tears it open. He rolls it down over his cock with quick, confident strokes as I settle back on the bed, staring up at him.

He moves between my thighs, spreading them open with his big hands as he gazes down at my flushed core.

"So fucking gorgeous," he murmurs, and it doesn't even seem like he's trying to talk dirty. He's speaking to himself more than anyone else, and he sounds almost... awed.

I blush a little, biting my lip. Jason went down on me from time to time—usually when he was hoping I'd return the favor by blowing him—but he definitely never took the time to just *look* at my pussy, and he never studied it like it was the most beautiful thing in the world.

Keeping his grip on my legs, North slowly starts to press into me. I can't help but watch, entranced by the way my body stretches around his thick cock. Raven and Cain are watching too, and somehow, that knowledge makes the moment feel exponentially hotter.

"You're tight," North groans as he bottoms out and pulls back to thrust again. "Did you squeeze my brothers like this? Did your greedy pussy clench around them like it never wanted to let them go?"

Cain makes a noise in his throat, and I get the feeling he's remembering what it felt like to be inside me. I whimper, my mouth falling open as North and I rock on the bed with every thrust. I don't know if his question was rhetorical or not, but I'm beyond the power of speech by this point.

I'm not sure I can come again, but every stroke of North's cock feels incredible. I can feel the beginnings of soreness, and I know I'll definitely feel this tomorrow, but I don't want it to ever stop.

Still sliding in and out of me, North releases my legs and drapes his upper body over mine, bracing himself to keep his weight from crushing me. We're skin to skin now, my breasts pressed against his chest as his chest hair scrapes the sensitive buds of my nipples.

"I watched your expression every time you came tonight," he whispers, his face so close to mine that his breath fans over my lips. "And I want to see it one more time. Can you come for me, sweet one? Can you let go one more time?"

I'm about to shake my head, since I really don't know if my overworked body can handle one more orgasm. But before I get the chance, heat begins to bloom low in my belly, as if North set off some kind of chain reaction with his words.

"Yes," I breathe. "Fuck. Yes. Just keep doing that. Keep..."

He does, thrusting a little harder so that pleasure shoots through my clit every time he bottoms out. I can feel tension building in his back and shoulders, the muscles turning hard as stone beneath my hands as they contract. He's close too, and it occurs to me in a rush that I want to see what he looks like when he comes, just like he saw with me.

I unwrap my arms from around his shoulders and reach up to frame his face with my hands, staring into his eyes as our bodies collide over and over.

And then it happens.

The deep black of his pupils expands into the dark blue of his irises, and his nostrils flare. His lips pull back in a grimace as a deep grunt pours from his lips, his neck muscles straining as he drives into me one last time and then grinds his hips against mine.

"Oh fuck," I whimper. "Fuck, I'm—"

My thighs clamp around his waist as the orgasm I wasn't sure I could even have swells inside me like a hurricane. It rips through my body, making my limbs shake, and I keep staring into North's eyes as the pleasure peaks and finally begins to ebb away, letting him see everything.

As the tension drains from both of us, he rests his forehead against mine, letting more of his body weight press into me. He's heavy, but it feels good. Grounding, in a way.

Warm breath tickles my ear, and I realize that Cain

and Raven are on either side of us. Once again, I'm surrounded by all three of these men, and the realization makes me grin sleepily.

"Thank you," I murmur. "That was the best antidote to a breakup *ever*. I honestly can't even remember what's-his-name's name. Although, to be fair, I can barely remember *my* name anymore."

"Good." Cain chuckles, nuzzling my hair. "That means we did our job right."

"Fuck yeah, you did." I laugh, tilting my head a little to kiss North. Then I turn to the right and then the left, kissing Cain and Raven too. I can taste all three of them on my tongue and smell their distinctly different scents mingling in the air around me.

North pulls out of me, securing the condom with one hand as he does. My skin is slicked with a sheen of sweat, and I feel warm and cozy.

And sleepy.

So fucking sleepy.

I don't know what the protocol is for mind-blowingly hot one-night stands after the sex part happens. I hadn't planned on staying the night—hadn't even thought that far ahead when we left the bar—but I'm too comfortable to muster up the energy to get up.

Lips pepper kisses over my skin as my eyes drift closed. Someone pulls a blanket over me, and I hear three deep voices murmuring quietly to each other, although I'm fading too fast to pick up what they're saying.

An arm wraps around me as someone spoons me from behind, and I feel another body settle into place in front of me.

Then sleep steals over me.

I wake up feeling amazing.

Well, to be fair, I sort of feel like I got hit by a truck, but in the best way possible.

Holy shit. I've never had sex that good.

My body is sore in places I never even knew existed until last night, but it's a good kind of ache, like the way you feel after a satisfying workout in the gym. I stretch a little, feeling my muscles groan in satisfaction as my clit throbs softly.

Hot damn. I didn't know that these kinds of things could happen outside of porn.

On top of that, I feel like a weight has been lifted. I feel freer, more relaxed. I guess that's what revenge sex against your cheating boyfriend will do for you. Or really good sex in general.

Man. Jason was decent in bed, but what happened last night was on a whole other level. Holy fuck.

I look around and realize I'm in a tangle of bodies. The guys are all still asleep, and it's hard to tell who's who and who's touching me since we're all so tangled up.

Now that they're asleep, they look less alpha, less dangerous—in a sexy way—softer and more vulnerable. It tugs at my heart, oddly. I kind of want to stay.

But what the hell am I thinking? I can't stay. That's not how one-night stands work. I had fun, and now it's time to go. I've stayed on top for this long by not letting anyone in, not even Jason, and that's all for the best. Jason proved last night why I'm right to keep people at arm's length. I don't know these guys at all.

Although, I can admit that I never really let Jason in. Maybe he cheated on me because he could feel that I was holding back on him?

Ugh, even if that's true, it's no excuse for how he cheated.

I slide out of bed, trying not to wake the men as I search for my dress on the floor. I start to look for my panties before I remember that they're still near the entry door, and the thought makes me grin as my cheeks heat up at the memory of how I lost them. I'm still pissed at Jason, but I'm glad as hell that I ended up in the bar last night and met these three.

Rather than leaving the room to get my panties first, I just tug the dress on over my head. But I must make too much noise rustling the fabric, because Raven rolls over onto his side, blinking his eyes open. I finish tugging my dress down as he looks over at me.

Shoot. I was sort of hoping to slip out without saying anything. Last night, I let all my inhibitions down, but in the cold light of morning, I'm not quite sure what to say to any of these men. How do you thank three guys for the best orgy of your life?

Well, the *only* orgy of my life, but the point still stands.

"Sorry! Go back to sleep," I whisper, sidling toward the door. "I didn't mean to wake you up."

"Where are you going?" He sounds sleepy and confused.

"Um... home?"

Where else would I be going?

"Why?" he asks.

"Oh, I just have a lot to do today," I mutter evasively, feeling like an idiot. I've never really had a one-night stand before, so I have no idea what kinds of things people usually say to each other the morning after.

How do people get out of the apartments of their hot hookups gracefully? God, I suck at this.

Our whispered conversation has woken the other two men up, and I flush as I realize they're giving me the same look Raven is. They don't seem upset, just confused as well, gazing at me like I've grown a second head.

Before I can come up with a better excuse for why I need to get going, North gets out of bed. He's still naked, and holy shit, it makes me remember last night vividly. I can feel heat spiking in me again, my heart rate picking up.

It takes a lot of work to keep my eyes on their faces, especially when Cain gets out of bed too, and the blanket slides down to reveal Raven's chest. They're so fucking hot. It's unfair. I have to keep myself from doing something stupid like kissing them again and starting round two—or round three... or four... I'm not sure.

"I was just, uh, telling Raven that I need to go home," I say lamely, trying to drag my thoughts back out of the gutter.

"But your home is here," North says.

Okay. That's weird. "No, my home is my apartment."

The men still look confused.

I shake my head. "Last night was incredible, don't

get me wrong. It was life-altering. Maybe we can see each other again sometime, but right now, I've gotta get going."

"But why would you leave?" Cain asks. "You're our mate."

I blink.

Their *what?*

CHAPTER 6

"I'm sorry." I can't quite believe what I just heard. "Your what?"

Mate? That's not a thing that exists, right? I mean, I think vampires and werewolves call their partners mates, right? But that's not... I'm so confused.

"You're our fated mate," North growls, confident. He looks like he's ready to stalk toward me and kiss me again, to prove with his body that we're fated. I'll be honest, if he does decide to seduce me, I'm not gonna be able to resist. I mean... whoo.

"Can't you feel it?" Raven asks. He sounds almost hurt that I can't feel whatever it is that he's feeling.

"Oh, I bet she can." Cain's smirking at me, his gaze dragging over my body. "Don't you, sweetheart?"

"I..." I swallow hard and look away. Fuck. I can't talk

with them while they're naked like this, looking like they want to devour me. I'm getting turned on, and I can't have a serious conversation like this. "Could you guys please put some clothes on?"

Cain chuckles, but all three of them start grabbing clothes. Thank fuck.

"We're all part fae," North explains, that growl still in his voice. "And our fae natures have formed a mate bond with you. We could sense it when we first walked into the bar. We assumed you did too."

"I'm going to be honest," I admit, "I didn't—you guys are just really, really sexy, and I was in a bad place after, you know, the whole boyfriend thing—I don't know anything about a mate bond."

Is this the kind of thing your fae parents are supposed to tell you about? Did I miss out on this vital information because they died and nobody could inform me? Or is this a rare random thing?

Cain shrugs nonchalantly. "Not surprising. Fated bonds are rare. They haven't really been a thing for a long time. As our numbers dwindled..." A look of anger and disgust crosses his face, and I know he's thinking about how the vampires nearly wiped us out. "...fated mates became less and less common."

"But now we have you, and you have us," Raven says. He walks over to me, staring at me like I'm the

Milky Way and he's just now seeing me for the first time. I have to admit, seeing such devotion is intoxicating.

All three men are looking at me, actually, and for a moment... I'm tempted. They're so handsome, and the sex was amazing. I want to stay and let them worship my body some more, let them make me feel as good as they did last night...

But I shake my head.

"I'm sorry, I can't stay." No matter how good the sex was, I just can't. I'm not ready to have one mate, let alone three. Being alone is what's kept me alive this entire time. "You guys are great, but..."

North's head shoots up, and he looks over my shoulder, nostrils flaring in alarm. A moment later, I hear tinkling glass, like something breaking.

"Someone's here," North growls.

A moment later, three men with their faces covered by ski masks burst into the room.

Fuck!

They're supernatural, definitely, and all three of them dive for me.

"Donovan says hello," one of them growls as he reaches for me. I dive out of the way on instinct, my mind racing as I process the name he just uttered.

How? How the fuck is this possible? I have a concealment charm.

But even as I have that thought, a horrible realization washes over me. When I was storming around getting all of my stuff from Jason's place after I realized he was cheating on me, my charm must've fallen off by accident.

Shit, shit, shit.

That charm was the one thing keeping me safe from the spells Donovan uses to try to find me. And now I'm going to—

A snarl erupts from my left side, and North leaps in front of me before the intruder can come after me again, snarling almost like a wolf. Cain and Raven immediately step up too, and Raven gently reaches out to pull me behind them. His skin looks... grayer now? Or am I just imagining that?

All three men look like they're ready to rip Donovan's goons limb from limb.

"There," Cain says, a smirk in his voice. "Now this is a fair fight."

Then, like a rubber band snapping, all six of the men in the room leap into motion.

My jaw drops open as chaos explodes in the small space.

They're fighting Donovan's lackeys. For *me*.

Nobody has ever stepped forward for me like that before, defended and helped me. And Jason really only proved that I can't trust anyone to ever do something like that for me. A guy couldn't even stay loyal to me. Why would I expect someone to get in between me and bloodthirsty, furious vampires?

But these three are jumping right into the fray and attacking these supernaturals with everything they have.

Well, like hell I'm going to let these guys have all the fun. This is *my* fight. I jump right in, ready to fight for my life.

These supernaturals are fighting hard, obviously aware of what'll happen to them if they go back to Donovan empty-handed after having me right in their grasp. But North, Cain, and Raven are more than a match for them. They're absolute blurs, attacking these supernaturals like their own lives are in danger and it's not just me.

I'm pretty fucking ruthless myself. Look, it's a dog eat dog world out there. And if anyone tries to come after me, I know there's only one solution here, only one way to fight. You don't fight for honor, or to win—you fight to *kill*. Because if you don't, your opponent sure might be, and they'll get the upper hand. I've never been able to afford to relax during a fight. There's never been anyone to back me up, so it's all on me to win.

Until now.

Raven seems to shift as he fights, his tattoos vanishing or changing and his skin going gray. He deals heavy punch after heavy punch, like he's in an underground fight club and he was told just to keep hitting until his opponent's a pulp. It's a heavy-handed, direct kind of fighting that I certainly wouldn't want to be on the receiving end of. You have to be strong as fuck to be able to fight like this, just straight-on slugging people.

There's a part of me that finds it kind of hot.

I dodge back out of the way as Raven goes after the guy, again and again, gaping as the attacker's blows bounce off Raven like trying to punch a tank.

Another one of the attackers lunges for me, trying to grab me, I think to try to drag me and portal us out of here. I dodge, his fingers just barely missing me, and I can feel the whip of the air moving across my skin created from the movement. I can't let them get a hold of me and portal me to Donovan. There's no way I could bargain for my life right now. I'm good, but I don't think I'm *that* good.

Cain grabs the guy's wrist, and immediately the man's arm sets on fire. The man screams, writhing, and Cain grabs the guy by the throat, and then *that's* on fire, too.

I back up, my hands in the air, my eyes feeling like they're bugging right out of my head. North is moving with lightning speed, kind of similar to Raven with sheer strength, but moving more like I'm used to seeing in fights, a combination of strength and skill and speed.

He's clearly had a lot of fight training and knows how to use his body, how to fight and *win, and I* find myself for the first time staring instead of helping out in a brawl.

I can't help myself. I've never seen people who were so capable at it. I learned from the school of hard knocks. I fight for my life and it taught me a lot. But wow.

Part of me is envious. I want to be as powerful of a fighter as these three are. I want to be completely badass like that, so that no bounty hunter would stand a chance against me.

Within minutes, the three men are dead on the floor, North, Cain, and Raven standing over them. All three men have snarls on their faces, like they're disgusted, like they can't believe someone would even try to attack me and think they could get away with it.

"Thank you," I blurt, not sure what else to say. They didn't have to do that for me.

Raven gives me that look again. "Of course."

"Why?" I can't help but ask. "Do you have any idea what kind of target is on your back now?"

"If a target is on your back," Cain replies, "then it's on our backs too, don't you know how it works, darling?"

"No, I don't know how it works," I snap. I know I'm

being a little cranky, but my heart is still pounding, and I can't quite believe that all of this is happening. How am I supposed to know how this works? I don't have anyone. I've never had anyone. How can I be expected to just accept this all as fact? How can I be expected to do an instant one-eighty?

"You're our mate," North growls. He reaches up and gently tucks some hair behind my hair. "That's what we do."

They sound like it's so obvious to them. Like they're having to remind me of gravity's existence, some universal law that of course I know about, silly, I just have to think about it for a moment.

"I'm not—" I'm not dragging them down with me, or roping them into my problems, I mean to say, but North interrupts me.

"Why were these men after you?" he asks.

Um. "I have a mob boss after me. Kind of a peril of the trade, you know. Sometimes you rub powerful people the wrong way."

North nods, then looks at the other two. "Then we'll help you get him off your back."

My mouth nearly drops open. "Are—you—"

To say that I'm shocked would be an understatement. I can feel my face flushing with heat.

Part of me wants to say no—I don't want to drag

BOUND TO THE DARK

these guys into it, and technically they're still strangers to me. How can I trust them? What if they're just going to set me up? You can't believe anyone in this world. That's the one thing I've learned since I was forced to make it on my own.

And yet... I feel innately as though I *can* trust them. I don't know how I know, I just... do. And they did just fight off these men for me.

"I can't turn down the help," I admit, folding my arms. "All right. You can help me."

"So magnanimous," Cain murmurs, sounding amused. He winks at me when I look over at him.

I look down at the men on the floor. To be honest... I'd been with Jason because he had seemed like a sweet, supportive guy. A *safe* guy. Someone who couldn't hurt me—but also someone who couldn't keep up with me. And I barely had to do anything in that fight just now. Those three were like whirlwinds, taking the men down before I could so much as blink.

"You don't believe that we're your mates," Raven says. He sounds sad, but like he's trying to hide it.

I feel bad, but I don't want to lie to him. "I'm sorry."

"Don't worry." North sounds confident. "You're letting us help you, and that's all we need. We'll prove ourselves worthy of being your mates."

"You guys sure are determined," I observe.

Cain and North smile at me. "We're going to prove it to you," North promises me. "You'll see."

Nobody's ever said anything like that to me before—saying they want to prove themselves worthy of me. In spite of myself, I'm feeling warm inside, feeling special.

"Okay, then," I tell them.

Let's give this a shot.

CHAPTER 7

First things first, we have to get rid of the bodies.

I've never had to deal with this kind of thing before. I rob people, but I'm not a damn murderer. I'm not used to this kind of thing. "Do we, um, dissolve them in the bathtub?"

Once on a TV show I saw someone do that. Or no, wait, they were supposed to cut the bodies up and dissolve them in plastic tubs, but the guy did it in the bathtub and the acid or whatever they used to dissolve the bodies ate through the bottom of the tub too and through the floor and made this huge mess.

North shakes his head. "No. We have a solution sort of on standby for this."

On standby? "Should I be concerned that you know

so easily how to take care of bodies that you have a solution ready to go?"

"We're not exactly as old as we look," North says, as Cain comes in with some rope. "We're much older. We've been around a while and we've had some run-ins. We figured it was best to be prepared."

"So are you... bounty hunters too?" What if their flirting with me and seduction of me was all this elaborate trap to win me over so that they could lead me to Donovan themselves?

"We've done a bit of that," North admits. "But we would never hurt you."

"You're our mate," Raven adds.

Cain starts tying up the bodies, and I raise an eyebrow at him.

"What, you think they're going to come back to life and start attacking again?" I ask.

He chuckles. "No, but tying them up makes them easier to carry. No limbs flailing around."

"Oh." I blink. "That... makes sense, I guess." I don't know what other response there is to what he just said other than *what the fuck*.

North opens a portal and each of the men takes a body, stepping through. I step through as well, following them. It might not be the smartest idea to follow three people I barely know to an undisclosed location, but I want to know what they're doing.

We step into a large, rather bare room with tiled walls and a concrete floor. There's some equipment, including metal gurneys, off to one side. Up against one wall is a massive furnace.

"We're at the local crematorium," Cain tells me, relaxed and nonchalant.

"You guys make use of the crematorium regularly?" I'm not sure if I'm asking seriously or if I'm joking around. I know next to nothing about these guys, and I feel safe with them—but I don't know if I can trust that safe feeling. I haven't felt safe around anyone in years.

"Oh, only about once a month or so," he replies, waggling his brows. He's clearly teasing me, and that helps relax me a little. I don't think he'd go so far as to lie if they did in fact use this portal regularly.

"The incinerator is the best place," North says, opening it up. I wince as the bodies are unceremoniously fed inside one at a time. They have to wait until one body is finished before they can put in another, and the smell isn't exactly pleasant.

"You have to get used to the smell," Cain says sagely, noticing my face of disgust.

"It's not a place that can be traced back to us," North

continues to explain, as if no interruption had occurred. "And even if someone did want to investigate, it'll be nearly impossible to find one particular person's remains among all the others that they put in here."

"You guys really know what you're doing," I admit.

"For how long we've been around, we'd better."

Once the bodies are finished being, well, burned, North opens the portal again and we step back through into their apartment. I think that was the trippiest thing I've ever done. And they're acting like it's completely normal. Just who have I gotten myself mixed up with?

And yet, I feel safe with them. I don't know what to do about that.

"Food," Raven says, and without further ado, he goes into the kitchen.

He seems to be a man of few words.

North looks me up and down, clinically, like he's my doctor. "You should get something to eat," he decides.

"Um, okay?" I pause. "Are you saying I'm too skinny?"

"I'm saying you look like you don't take care of yourself enough," North replies. "All work and no relaxation."

Damn it, he's got me there.

I follow the three men into the rather lovely kitchen.

I have to admit, this apartment of theirs is nice. Not that I really got the chance to appreciate it last night. I was busy appreciating other things. But now in the morning light I can actually see around me and it looks like a place that people have really made a proper home.

The walls of the kitchen are painted a bright and sunny yellow, with cream-colored cabinets and a retro style fridge. The living room's blue, with cream-colored bookshelves stuffed with all kinds of books. There seem to be a few different genres—action thriller, mystery, historical fiction, and nonfiction. And the works of Jane Austen.

"The Austen is mine," Cain says, following my gaze. "So is all the historical fiction. Raven likes action, seeing if he can solve the mystery and guess who the killer is. North is boring. He likes nonfiction."

"I like educating myself," North counters.

"What about you?" Cain asks me.

"I was always big into science fiction," I reply. The truth is, I haven't sat down and relaxed with a good book in ages. It's one of those things where I always mean to get into it but then I never have the time. There's always something else to do.

"Well, if you want to borrow anything," Cain says, "feel free."

"Thanks." They're just... offering their home up to me so easily? Who does that?

There are some more books piled on the coffee table in the middle of the room, all apparently in French. There are knights on the covers, though, so I'm pretty sure these are Cain's. On the opposite wall is a large television, flanked on either side with a Van Gogh print. Below it is another set of shelves, these all filled with a record collection.

I point. "Whose are these?"

"Mine," North says.

"Nice." Looks like a mix of blues, jazz, and classic rock.

These three obviously have wildly different personalities. How do they all get along so well? And how am I wildly attracted to all three of them when they're so different?

None of them stop me as I continue to wander around the space. There's a lot more room there than at my apartment, obviously, since I have a studio, but that's not what's tripping me up. It's the strong sense of *home* that this place has.

"We've done a lot of modifications over the years," Cain says. "Put in magical security measures, reinforced some things... knocked out a wall..."

"Did your landlord let you?"

Cain grins. "He was persuaded."

"Cain's very persuasive," North mumbles.

I don't keep a whole lot of stuff in my own apartment. You never know when you might have to pack up because of the police or getting on the wrong side of a supernatural being. And I couldn't let anything show that revealed my true fae nature. Just in case someone like Jason came over. After losing everything when my parents were killed and then being on the streets, the idea of having a lot of stuff around that I might have to then carry with me or abandon made me panic.

But these three... I like what they've done. I like this place. It feels like a home and it's only now that I'm looking around inside one that I realize how much I crave one of my own. That I want to walk into a place and think, *oh, yes, I belong here.*

"You like pancakes?" Raven asks, getting ingredients out of the cupboards and fridge. He startles me out of my reverie, and I jump a little, turning around to look back toward the kitchen.

"Um, sure?" I can't remember the last time I had pancakes.

Raven's going all out, too. He's not grabbing the

quick pancake mix, he's actually getting out eggs and flour, the whole shebang. I look over at North and Cain.

"He likes to cook," North says, as if this explains everything.

Maybe it does, for them. I've never had a one-night stand make me breakfast before. Although, to be fair, the main reason for that is because I've never had a one-night stand at all until now, so I don't really know what the breakfast expectations are. But Jason sure as hell never made me breakfast.

As I watch, Raven goes to the fridge and pulls out eggs and bacon, then gets some coffee brewing. Wow.

"What do you want to know about us?" Cain asks, sitting down at the table and gesturing for me to join him. The apartment's an open floor plan—there's the front door, with the kitchen area immediately to the right, and then immediately to the left is the bathroom and bedroom. Ahead is the open area that's divided into the living room with the books and TV, and then a dining area with a large oak table.

I sit down gingerly, taking the seat diagonal to Cain. "What do you mean?"

I don't know what mate rituals or whatever usually entail, but I'm not going to care what their astrological sign is or if they have enough cows to be worthy of being my mates.

"Well, you'll want to know about what kind of people your mates are," Cain says, his tone playful but patient. Probably more patient than I would be in this situation, if I was in his shoes.

"Um... sure." I try not to sound too eager. I want to know more about them. There's a kind of burning curiosity in my chest that I can't recall ever feeling before. But I'm not going to let them know about that.

"We're all hybrids," Cain explains. He gestures at himself. "Half fae, half demon."

Well, that explains the charm and charisma. Most people think of demons as these big disgusting hellish monsters and they're right about some of them, but the job of demons is also to tempt people into sinning, and you can't do that if you're slobbering lava all over someone. There are demons that are incredibly charming and seductive, and Cain's demon parent must have been one of those.

"North here is half shifter." Cain pauses. "Wolf, to be exact."

Shifters are, well, basically were-whatever, as humans call them. So North is, by human terminology, half werewolf. Shifters, however, can turn whenever they want. They're not bound by the cycles of the moon, and they're not turned into what they are by biting, and they can't bite someone else and make them transform. You're either born a shifter or you're not.

"And Raven, our chef de cuisine, is half gargoyle."

I think my mouth drops open. I've never heard of a half gargoyle before. That has to be rare, right? I quickly school my face into a neutral expression. It explains why Raven's skin seemed to turn gray as he was fighting those men just a few minutes ago, though. That must have been his gargoyle side coming out.

Honestly, I don't know much about gargoyles, how they act, what their society is like. I thought they were rather solitary creatures.

"H-how does that work?" I ask, unable to stop myself.

Raven turns off the stove and looks over at me. In the morning sunlight, in just a tank top and gym shorts, I can see almost all of his body in a way I couldn't last night. The blue-black hair, the swirling tattoos that climb up and over his limbs like vines, his gleaming eyes—no wonder he looks otherworldly to me, someone who's fae and used to other supernatural creatures. I've never seen his like before.

Raven shifts, his skin turning gray, his broad, muscled form becoming even bigger, hulking, claws growing out, horns spiraling up out of his head, fangs jutting out from his lips.

Then he shifts back, and he looks like his human—well, close to human—self again.

"There," he says, and I can see pink dusting his cheeks as he turns the stove on. He was embarrassed to transform for me? Or nervous? Maybe he thought I wouldn't like it.

"Very impressive," I tell him.

Raven's blush deepens. Okay, I have to admit, that's cute. And I'm thinking that a guy who can bench press three of me is cute, now that's a cause for concern. I can't get attached to these men, or attached to anyone. If you get attached, then you can get hurt and disappointed—or people can use that against you as a weakness. I can't let that happen.

"What about you?" Cain asks.

"Me? Oh. I'm full fae." I pause. "Or at least—I think I am. My parents were killed by vampires when I was a kid so I don't know a lot of my family history."

To try to protect ourselves, and to keep our population going in some way despite our small numbers, a lot of fae have married people from other races. We're the most cross-bred, ah, to use a bit of an antiquated term, out of all the supernatural creatures. So it's not all that surprising I'm dealing with three hybrids right now. I might also be a hybrid, but if I am it's from pretty far back. I don't have any special powers or traits.

"Vampires?" That distinctive growl is back in North's voice. Now I know what it means. "Fuckers."

"They'd wipe us all out if they had the chance," Cain adds.

"Things have been different," Raven points out. He slides some delicious-looking pancakes onto a plate, and I can smell bacon sizzling. Damn. I'm really getting pampered. "Ever since the king married... what's her name. She's part fae. He's been trying to crack down on vampires attacking fae."

Cain snorts. "I'll believe it when I see it. What have vampires ever done to make us trust them? We're supposed to think that everything is fine and dandy now?"

"Doesn't matter." North looks at me, then glances away, his voice low and gruff. "We'll protect you. You don't ever have to worry about vampires as long as you're our mate."

Raven sets a plate in front of me. It's got pancakes, bacon, and eggs. Then there's a bowl of fruit. My mouth falls open a little again. "Thank you."

Raven blushes and mumbles, "Of course." As if it's natural that he'd do this for me.

"Are you related?" I ask. If they're all half fae it could very well be that they share a parent who was just... friendly.

The three men all look at each other, and then Cain chuckles. "No, but I can see why you'd think that. We've been friends and working together for years. It made sense for us to stick together. Fae have to protect each other. It's so much easier than being alone."

That makes a lump form in my throat. I wouldn't know about that. In my experience, being alone is the easier option. Even if that does mean I've had to look over my shoulder a lot. But would I not have to do that, with them? Could they really take care of me like they're saying they would? Can I trust their word?

"None of us really had a clan or a pack," Cain goes on. "Shifters are... well. Anyway. Demons are rather self-serving so I couldn't expect much from that side of my family and gargoyles are rare so we all just decided why not? And we do have fun together."

He winks at me, and I can feel my face heating up. I know exactly what kind of fun he's talking about, after all.

I'm curious what Cain meant about shifters. They're notoriously tight knit. Why wouldn't they welcome a new member? Why wouldn't North be raised by the shifter side of his family, the pack he was born into? Do they dislike the fae side of him?

"So what's the deal with this mobster?" Cain asks.

I look over at North and Raven. North is tearing into

his pancakes but he has one eye on me. Raven's staring at me like he's... like he's staring at the stars. I'm not sure what to do with that.

I dig into my food to give myself some time. Fuck, this shit tastes delicious.

"Um." They're being honest with me and the truth will out sooner or later, so what's the harm in telling them at this point? I don't think they'll turn me in. "So the guy who's after me is Donovan O'Shae."

"The vampire?" Cain's eyes go wide.

North chokes on his pancakes and Raven has to thump him on the back.

"Shit." Cain shakes his head. "Of all the people you could get on the bad side of..."

"Trust me, I know." I rub my forehead. "I didn't know who he was. I mean, I knew who he was, who doesn't? But I didn't know that it was *him*. That he was the person I was stealing from. I was desperate, I've got student loans, and I thought—doesn't matter. I stole from him and now I have to replace it. It's the only thing I can think of to get him off my back."

"I'm not sure that'll be enough," Cain admits.

"It will be," Raven says with staunch loyalty.

"Stealing from someone like that and getting away with it?" Cain shakes his head. "Even if she returns it, he might want to kill her just to teach everyone else a lesson. With guys like that—their power comes from their reputation. They can't be seen as soft."

"It's not soft," I snap as worry claws at my throat. "It's fair. I'm returning what I stole and so there's no harm done. I'll even throw in a favor for him or something, but I can't do that until I actually return the thing or he'll never listen to me. I had a concealment charm to keep myself safe, but I've lost it and now it's only a matter of time until his goons or some other bounty hunters come after me."

I finish off the rest of my food and wait for the other shoe to drop. Now they know it's not some regular, human mob boss after me—it's one of the most dangerous and criminal vampires in the city. Far too much trouble for these men or anyone to deal with. They won't want to get caught in the crosshairs. They'll tell me they're sorry, maybe hook me up with a new concealment charm if they know someone, and then they'll send me on my way.

"Sounds like we need to get on it, then," North says.

I can't help but stare at him. "What?"

"I said, sounds like we need to get on it." North finishes up his food and pushes his plate away. "What did you steal?"

"An Aurora Gem," I admit, wincing.

"We'll get you a new concealment charm," Cain

says. "That'll buy us some time. Then we can help you find the gem."

"Are—are you sure? You know what you're up against. Or, um, who you're up against."

"You're our mate," Raven says, as if that explains everything.

And, well, to them, maybe it does.

CHAPTER 8

After breakfast, we head out to the underground market hidden under the Tin Cat. The Tin Cat is one of those places that's a front for something else, but they actually do make a mean cocktail. There are a lot of these places all over the city, supernatural stores or bars that actually serve as doorways to keep the larger parts of our world hidden from humans who could stumble upon it. Unless you know which bathroom stall to go into at the Tin Cat, and how to use it, you're not going to get into the market.

We nod at the bartender. It's daytime, so there's only a couple people seated in the actual bar part, day drinkers, retirees. We all have to cram into the stall in the men's room, and I can feel their bodies pressing up against me. Heat flashes through me, and I swallow.

Thing is, I don't know if it's just lust, or something more.

Cain puts his hands on my hips to steady me as the door opens and North steps through. Even though Raven's bigger than he is, and Cain's the charming talker, North is clearly the leader.

I step up behind North, peering over his shoulder, and holy shit, this place is huge. I've never been to this market before. I'm... well. I'm a college student at a human university. I try to stay away from too much of the supernatural world. Otherwise shit gets blurry. It's easier just to go cold turkey.

But this is amazing. There's rows and rows of stalls, and the smells and sounds almost overwhelm me. I can't tell where to look next. I want to take it all in. There's a stall piled high with colorful spices, and another with strange animals hanging from the ceiling and a large grill for roasting them.

"Your eyes are going to fall out of your head," Cain notes with a chuckle, his voice low and warm, his mouth right by my ear. "You never been here before?"

I shake my head. "I kind of distanced myself from the supernatural community."

Cain clucks his tongue. "Now that's a damn shame. No wonder we hadn't seen you around before."

He sounds like he's teasing, but also a little sad, like he's genuinely disappointed that they hadn't met me earlier.

North looks around, inhaling deeply, like he's taking in all the scents. He can probably identify all the smells, and know them better than I do. "This way."

Raven tucks me into his side, as if to protect me. Normally I'd wiggle away if someone tried to put his arm around me like this, but Raven's touch isn't too tight or confining. And I can't afford to reject protection, not until I get a new concealment charm on me.

Besides, I suppose there are worse things in this world than being next to a handsome guy like Raven. As the four of us move through the stalls, it's clear that the men are recognized. People smile and nod at them as they pass, or move out of the way to give them room.

All around us there's so much happening, I can hardly take it all in. My job is stealing unusual and expensive things for people, and this place is full of insane, creative magical items. Everywhere I look, there's something new.

There are women selling colorful scarves, potions, elixirs, and magical spices for food. There are jewelry stands everywhere, and piles of uncut gems for use in magical spells—or for eating, depending on what kind of supernatural creature you are. People of all genders are hawking their wares, while a man stands in the middle of a sort of square with a pile of maps in his hand, giving directions about which stall is where. It's like a farmer's market, a county fair, and a bazaar all rolled into one.

I walk up to a stall that has amulets hanging from the top of it and large crystal balls resting on the table. Some of them are smoky, some seem to have an eye in the middle, and still others are brightly colored. Along with the traditional clear ones, of course.

The next stall after that is selling chocolates, and I would normally just walk right up and buy some, but I doubt these are normal chocolates. Sure enough, when I read the little cards at the front of each row of chocolates that say what they are, I find out that one chocolate is supposed to induce a craze of lust inside you, and another is supposed to get you in a state of mind to be more receptive to learning about your past lives. There are even some chocolates that say they're specifically for only one type of supernatural creatures or other, like goblins or shifters.

Children run past me, chasing each other, and I grin. One of them is covered in scales and another appears to be a full fae, with delicate wings sprouting out of their back. They're yelling about another stall, and when I follow them, I see that this stall has a bunch of glowing butterflies the size of my face.

There aren't just butterflies, I see upon a closer look. There are dragonflies and moths and bumblebees. All of them are glowing slightly, and flap their wings slowly. They're obviously not actually real creatures, but constructs of some kind, but they look so lifelike, I have to reach out and touch one to make sure. It's delightful.

I turn back to make sure the men are still with me, and find that all three of them are looking at me with soft looks on their faces. Cain's straight-out smiling while North and Raven's faces just look like they've softened a bit, a warm light in their eyes.

"What?" I ask. I walk over to them, smiling a bit, feeling on the spot. "What is it?"

"Nothing," Cain says. "You're just adorable."

I can feel my face heating up. I'm a tall girl, nobody ever calls me adorable. And even if I was short, I don't think most people would call me that. I don't exactly give off warm and fuzzy feelings.

But none of the men are looking at me like they think I'm some cute creature that can't take care of herself. Instead they actually look delighted with me. Like I'm a field of summer flowers when they've been in the dark and snowy woods for months.

My heart warms at that, and I'm not sure what to do with it. "Um. Thank you?"

North barks out a laugh. Raven ducks his head down, trying and failing to smother a smile.

"You're welcome," Cain says. He sounds incredibly amused.

I can't help but bristle a little. I feel like I'm a bit behind. Like this is something that they all know, and I don't. Like I'm a child compared to them. They all know about this market and have probably been here a hundred times and yet this is my first time.

"You know that I'm perfectly capable of taking care of myself, right?" I ask. "I'm not a child you have to babysit and do the whole—I can show you the world thing from *Aladdin*."

"We just think it's nice, that's all," Cain says, putting a hand up like he's stopping me from moving forward. "It's all old hat to us. With you it's all new again and we get to see the... the fun in it once more."

North nods in agreement. "It's getting a new perspective."

Hmm. I hadn't thought of it that way. I wonder how much these men have seen in their lives and all that they've gone through. I know I have my own scars, and I can't help but want to know what theirs are.

Raven puts his arm around me again, looking around. "We need to get moving."

I want to just take my time and explore without a purpose, see what all there is, sampling things, buying whatever I want—but that'll have to wait for another day, when I'm not on a time crunch.

"We'll have to bring you back here," Cain observes, chuckling.

Raven nods at North, who nods back and turns to lead us again. Now that he's snapped back into focus, everything else seems to fade away. I watch as he picks up the scent again or whatever it is that he's focusing on, his nostrils flaring and eyes narrowing. He's like a dog that's picked up a scent, a man on a mission, and he unerringly leads us through the various 'streets'.

Cain seems to know a lot of people. He's waving and smiling at people as he walks by, calling out to them by name, and people call out to him in return and wave. Raven and North ignore them, but nobody seems offended. It's probably par for the course.

"It's good to get everyone on your side," Cain murmurs, leaning in so that he can speak almost right into my ear. "That way when the shit hits the fan, you can count on people to help you out or at least cheer you on instead of the other guy."

"Smart tactic." I've always been a loner myself, but I

suppose that there's a plus side to being open and friendly. Sure not my tactic, though.

We go down the twisting, winding 'streets', following North. They're not streets, exactly, but I don't know what else to call them. As we go, we're heading away from the main center of the market and toward the outskirts. I can't see the walls or ceiling of this underground place so I'm only going based on what is around us, and the noise and the bright colors are dying away to leave room for more serious stalls.

The people here aren't yelling out at us about their wares or showcasing fun trinkets. Instead, stalls seem to be about more serious matters. There's one stall that has a sign for wing operations. Another stall has a table that's just covered in different types of bones, all neatly laid out on display, and even several jars that are full of bone dust.

"Is this where all the dark magic lives?" I whisper, only half-joking.

"Magic isn't really dark or light," Cain replies, also quiet. "It's more about how you use it that makes it good or bad. Magic just is. You can use bones to curse someone or to heal someone. It's more like this is where people come for serious work or for help with a big problem rather than for a lighthearted shopping spree."

"That makes sense." I pause. I hate to admit my

insecurities. My weaknesses. Partially because I'm used to relying on myself and so I can't be weak because I have nobody else to lean on. Partially because if I admit to a weakness, that person can then use it against me. "I don't know much about magic. How it works. I just know magical items because of my work stealing them." I grin at him. "I could tell you how much just about anything in this market is worth."

"I bet you could." Cain sounds amused.

"Don't sell yourself short," Raven says quietly. "You know more than you think you do."

I'm startled by him speaking up, but not in a bad way. Raven has such faith in me, I want to demand that he give up on it. That I'm going to let him down if he keeps insisting on viewing me like that.

"Here we are," North says, his voice a soft growl. He stops in front of a particular stall, and the rest of us follow.

The stall is a little darker than the others. It has tapestries that fall down on the sides so that you can't quite see inside. I've noticed a few other stalls like that scattered here and there, but I didn't go up to them, and I don't know what they are. There isn't a sign indicating what it is, but North walks up to it and raps on the table.

A wizened old man with tattoos all over his face and arms greets us—or rather the guys. "Didn't think I'd be seeing you all back so soon." He pushes up the massive sleeves of the colorful blue-and-purple robe he's wearing. "What can I do for you guys?"

I wouldn't call these three 'guys' by any means, but then, I'm not ancient like this guy seems to be. He's clearly a magic-user of some kind. I'm pretty damn sure those tattoos on his skin have magical properties. You have to be careful around magic users. I've never particularly trusted them. They've always got their own agenda and they don't necessarily hold any loyalty toward any group.

At least, in my experience.

Raven must sense my apprehension, because he keeps his arm around me, stroking my skin lightly with his thumb, as if to soothe me. He doesn't talk as much as the other two, but I'd have to be blind, deaf, and an idiot to miss how ready he is to be my mate. It's oddly comforting, but also worrying. I'm not sure what to do in the face of such devotion.

"Always a pleasure to see you," Cain says, smiling in that charming way of his. "Is one of those tattoos new?"

"Now, now, sir, don't think I don't know what you're doing," the man responds, wagging his finger at Cain. He seems friendly enough. Or at least he seems comfortable with these three.

Cain laughs. I can't tell if he's comfortable with the

guy or not, or what he's thinking. Cain seems to be everyone's friend. But is it real? Or is it an act?

"We need a concealment charm," North says. He's not quite growling now, but his voice is firm.

The old man chuckles. "Now that's got a story behind it, I'm sure. You three just can't seem to avoid getting into trouble, can you?"

That makes me curious—what other things have these three gotten into?

Before I can ask, North replies. "It's none of your business why we need it."

"All right, all right." The man puts his hands up, shrugging. "Didn't mean to hit a sore spot. Who's it for?"

I raise my hand and the man beckons me closer while North glares at him as if to say *don't try any funny business*.

"Hold out your arm, would you?"

I do as I'm told, while the man waves his hands over my arm, muttering. I can't see anything, but it feels as though he's pricked my arm and is draining something out of me. I'm not all that nervous about it—the same thing happened when I got my last concealment charm. If you want them to be really effective, you need them to be specific to you, not just a general charm.

"This is going to be a high price," the man warns us.

"Money's not an issue," North says at once, pulling out his wallet.

"Whoa, whoa—" I reach out to try to stop him, but Raven squeezes me gently.

"We got this," he tells me. His voice and face are so soft, like it's not even a question of whether or not I'm going to let them pay, it's just the way things are.

"I can pay for this."

"It's not about whether or not you can," North growls, handing the man some money. "Let us take care of you."

What the hell am I supposed to do with this?

The man takes North's money, nodding. "I have her signature so I can create the charm. It'll be about fifteen minutes."

"Do you want to look around?" Cain asks as the man goes to make the charm in the back of his stall.

North grunts. "We should stay here."

"You guys really didn't have to do that for me. I lost my concealment charm, it's my own fault, and I brought trouble to you guys. It's not like you broke it or anything."

Cain sighs, then reaches up to tuck some of my dark hair behind my ear, his fingertips brushing along the curve of it. It makes me shiver with heat, even at such a small, delicate touch. "You darling creature, when are you going to figure out that we're going to take care of you? You're our mate, that's how it works."

I'm not sure what to make of Cain's charm—is he serious in calling me something like 'darling creature'? Or is it just a part of all... the demonic veneer that's in his blood?

"Once we get the charm," North adds, probably thinking I'm upset that I can't go shopping, "we can look around and you can get whatever you want."

You can get whatever you want implies that they'll be paying for whatever it is I'm going to get. What the hell. This whole thing is weird and kind of terrifying. I'm realizing that I have power over these men. I could ask for anything, and I'm pretty sure they'd get it for me. I don't know what the hell I'm supposed to do with this power. I don't want to abuse it.

But at the same time, it's not exactly— uncomfortable? It feels comforting, reassuring, even though I've only known them for barely a day. I can hardly believe that it's been so short of a time.

I open my mouth to protest that they will not be buying me anything else—I'm still an independent girl, and I have my own money, thanks—when North's head shoots up again and his eyes go dark, like a wolf who sees a rabbit.

"Shit," Raven mutters, shoving me behind him.

An instant later, a man lands right where I'd just been standing. From the stalls around us, four more people leap out—various supernaturals, one a transformed shifter in full wolf mode.

Shit indeed. More assassins have found me.

CHAPTER 9

The transformed shifter lets out a howl, and all around us everyone dives for cover. They probably don't know what's going on, but they sure as hell know a fight when they see one.

North growls and leaps at the guy, tackling him to the ground as Raven transforms, his claws, fangs, and horns emerging, his skin going gray. He's even bigger now, and he looks like something you wouldn't want to meet down a dark alley. It's reassuring to know that he's on my side.

Three of the assassins come for me, and Raven grabs all of them with his massive clawed hands, roaring, sending them crashing in a tangle into one of the stalls.

One of the assassins hits me from the side, sending

the two of us flying. I'm airborne for just a second as my feet leave the ground, and I grab onto the pole from one of the stalls that's used to hold up the canopy, using my momentum to spin around the pole and kick my attacker in the face.

The guy's face is distorted—all of the assassins' faces are—it's clearly a magical charm of some kind to make sure that nobody can recognize them later. It's like a real-time version of when television shows blur out a person's face for interviews.

He's disoriented from the kick, so I punch him right in the face—I can feel his nose crunching, and I feel a surge of triumph. Ha!

The guy goes down, but then someone grabs my arm. I whip around, and I see it's the magic user—wizard, magician, whatever—and he's waving his other fingers in the air in a spell that is definitely *not* for a concealment charm.

Yeah, I'm pretty sure we know how the assassins found me. Fuck's sake.

There's a slithering, hissing growl, not like a wolf growl, almost like if a snake learned to make proper noise, and Cain's there, grabbing the magician's wrist, snarling like—well, like a demon.

"Traitor," he spits. His eyes are glowing and blood starts to seep out from where he's holding onto the other man, red staining the tattoos on his arms.

The magician's face contorts with fear as he realizes what Cain is. "P-please, I'm sorry, the bounty on her is—it's huge, I didn't know—I didn't know she had friends like you—"

The shadows around Cain seem to distort, and he almost seems taller now. Like he's drawing the darkness into him and making it a part of his body. "You filthy, squirming little—"

"Cain!" North growls, a reprimand. "We have to go."

Cain glares at the man like he wants to finish what he started, but he releases him. The magician cowers, his arms up in front of his face, shaking.

I've gotta admit, it gives me some real satisfaction to see him like this. Ha. I've never been able to scare anyone who's wronged me like that before. I should probably feel scared of Cain, of his demonic side, but I just feel safe. He was using it to protect me—and I just know, innately, that he'd never hurt me.

Cain takes my hand, looking perfectly normal again, and leads me to rejoin the other two. The other assassins are lying on the ground, or seem to have vanished. Raven looks normal again, and North has some blood on him.

"We need to go," North says. "Before they get another read on us."

"Go where?" I ask.

Where, apparently, is a safe house that the guys have. It's near the market, in an abandoned subway tunnel.

We tear out of the market, dodging through stalls. My instinct is to slow down and walk. "We can't make ourselves look conspicuous!" I point out.

"Speed over subtlety," Cain says, keeping a hold of my hand so we stick together as we weave through the crowd. "We have to get you concealed as soon as possible."

He looks over his shoulder at me, grinning. "Why, you get into a lot of chases?"

"Not in a while." Not since I got good enough that I could be hired to steal fancy things from fancy apartments as opposed to pickpocketing.

Cain looks ahead again, and we continue to zip through the stalls and the crowd. We get back to the busier section of the market and we dodge the people, trying to move while also avoiding knocking into anyone. There are a few near-misses as I nearly trip over running kids or some unfortunate timing means we nearly crash into someone laden with purchases.

At least here, in the main hub of the market where everyone seems to be, any bounty hunters that appear will try to tail us rather than just attack. Donovan's powerful, but I'm not sure he's powerful enough to have everyone looking the other way if there's a fight in the middle of the market. Authorities would be called in for sure, not to mention the mess it would make.

Most criminals like a clean getaway. Myself included.

This is far from a clean getaway. We're running until my lungs burn, back up to the entryway, and then out through the bar.

"Watch it!" the bartender yells at us as we dash back through.

North leads us out onto the streets and then right down a subway entrance. Thank fuck there are a million of these in New York City. You just turn a corner and bam, there's another one.

We head down the steps, and then hop on a train, getting off at another station I don't even recognize. North leads us onto another platform—and then comes the not-fun part.

North jumps down onto the tracks after a subway car's passed, then reaches up to grab me and help me down.

For once, I accept the help. I'm nervous. What if we time this wrong and get hit?

Cain and Raven jump down next, and we hurry into the darkness. Almost immediately, North finds an entryway to another tunnel and enters it. For a second, it's like he's vanished into thin air, walked right into a wall.

I follow with Cain's gentle pushing, stepping through the narrow gap that quickly widens into the long-abandoned tunnel.

"How did you find this?" I ask, following North as he purposefully heads down this tunnel. I get the feeling he could get us there with his eyes closed.

"There are plenty of abandoned places down here," Cain says. "So we got subway maps and building plans from various years and cross-referenced them to get a list of tunnels that were abandoned. Then we did some searching to find the place that would best suit us."

"No offense," North says, "but you're not the first time we've had to camp out in a safe house."

Did serious North just make a joke? I smile at him. "You mean I'm not the first person to fall into your laps and cause trouble? I feel so cheap and used now."

North chuckles quietly.

"What sort of trouble have you gotten into?" I ask. "That you've had to... camp out?"

"We haven't always had the safest jobs," North says. "Sometimes fulfilling a job would anger someone else.

Or a job would go wrong, no fault of ours, but the client didn't see it that way. Or we'd be brought into a job where we weren't given all the facts, and once we had them, we tried to back out. Nobody liked that, either."

"We were bounty hunters," Cain says. "Among other things. We've done our share of unsavory things. But we have our code, and we stick to it."

I sense that they're not ready to tell me more. I'm wildly curious. I want to know more about these jobs they've done. They've obviously led very interesting lives. Who wouldn't want to know more? But I want to respect their privacy. If I'm not ready to spill my life story to them, why should I expect them to share theirs with me?

Also, why do I even care? I don't care. I don't. Who cares about other people's lives? What matters is keeping my own head above water. I've never wanted to know someone's life story before. Why should I start now?

Why do I care so much?

North stops at last and walks up a couple of short concrete steps to a large steel door. It's nondescript, utilitarian, but also very obviously there.

But I couldn't see it until North walked up to it.

"This was supposed to be some kind of operation room," Cain explains as North gets the door open and leads us inside. "But we spruced it up."

"Magical wards everywhere," North says. "It's concealed."

Excellent. As long as I stay in here, it's as good as wearing a concealment charm.

Of course, I can't stay in here forever.

"You can't even see the door unless you're one of the approved people," Cain goes on. "Or if you're with the approved people, like you're with us. Once we point out the door to you, you can see it, but not until then."

Very clever. "I should've tricked out my apartment like this."

Of course, I can't imagine how much work and money this cost. It would've taken them ages. I could never afford to make my apartment like this. Especially since I was avoiding magic, and I didn't want anything permanent. I still don't. I'm ready to go at the drop of a hat.

But it makes me wonder, once again, how powerful are these guys? Just who are these men that claim they're my mates?

Once we get inside, I see that it is a safe house, literally. I expected some kind of bunker-like situation, but instead, it's like I've walked into a studio apartment. There's a large bed in one corner, a kitchen against the opposite wall, and a dining room table. It's not as homey and decorated as the apartment I woke up in, but that's understandable if the guys aren't here often.

All in all, it's cozier than I expected. I like it.

"You can stay here. We've got food and everything," North says. "We keep it stocked. If you're fae, you never know when you might have to run."

True. We're used to being hunted.

"Donovan will probably have people looking for you now," I point out. "Everyone in the market saw you defending me and killing his assassins. You're on his hit list now too."

"It doesn't matter," Raven says. "You're our mate. We're sticking by you. He was going to find out about us eventually. Someone threatens you, they threaten us, too. That's how it works."

My heart warms, and I have to look away, overwhelmed. "Well. I can't be here for too long. Donovan will find it eventually. And without a charm I can't go out to find a gem."

"We don't need to go searching for an Aurora Gem," North says, and he gets a mischievous spark in his eyes.

"What do you mean?"

North nods at Cain and Raven.

"We can use our Sight to find an Aurora Gem for you," Cain says, sounding pleased as punch that he has a solution for me. "Raven and I can, I mean."

"Are you serious?"

The men nod at me, like it's the most obvious thing in the world. "Here," Cain says, walking over to the couch. "We'll show you."

He and Raven sit on the couch, Raven's tattoos shining a little—and then it's almost like his tattoos *shift*.

Cain's eyes go white. So do Raven's. It's like they're blind. I have to admit that it's pretty startling to watch.

North puts a hand on my shoulder. "Don't worry," he says, his voice low and soothing. "They're okay."

"I've never seen someone use the Sight before," I admit. "I didn't really grow up in the fae community."

"It's not something that most fae would do around others anyway," North replies. "It can be very intimate. Especially if you're looking at your own life. Instead of just trying to search for something."

"It's... more disconcerting than I expected."

North squeezes my shoulder. "I know. The first time I saw a fae do it, I thought they were having a seizure. But they're good at this. They know how to handle themselves."

"They won't... I've heard of fae that got stuck somehow. Or went mad."

North snorts. "Those were fae that didn't know what was good for them. Cain and Raven aren't like that.

They know their limits. They're not trying to unlock the future or read an entire past life."

I suppose so. I still feel off-kilter about it. It's just disconcerting to watch the two men as they sit there. They're barely even breathing, still as statues. If I just walked into the room and found them like this, I'd have a bit of a heart attack.

"You want anything?" North asks. "To drink, I mean?"

He sounds a bit awkward, for the first time a little off-kilter instead of the confident leader that I've seen him be the rest of the time. It's kind of endearing, actually.

I shake my head. "No, I'm okay."

North nods. "I usually count on Cain to do the small talk."

"No shit, I hadn't noticed."

He snorts in amusement, looking at me out of the corner of his eye. Yeah. It's sweet.

Cain and Raven sit perfectly still for about twenty minutes, and then Raven's tattoos shift again, and their eyes go back to normal.

"Okay," Cain says, looking over at Raven, who nods. "We've got a starting place. We've seen a vision of the building where the Aurora Gem is being held." He looks over at North. "We'll need to do more research before we can leave the safe house, figure out the location of the building, but it's a start."

I have to admit, that's pretty damn helpful. If they have a building, that's a lot more than I've been able to get over the last few weeks as I've scrambled for a gem.

For the first time, I'm starting to actually feel hopeful.

CHAPTER 10

The safe house has a bathroom, so I take a shower while the guys settle in. It's going to be tight quarters, and I'm tempted to tell them that I'll take the couch, but I doubt they'll accept that answer.

This bathroom is nice, I have to admit. There are three towels hanging up, one red, one blue, and one green. I'm guessing the green is North's and the blue is Raven's. The red is obviously Cain's. Even this safe house, cozy as it is, is all tricked out and lovingly decorated. Lots of care went into this place.

There's even a little painting by the bathroom mirror. It shows a sailboat on the ocean, I think up in Cape Cod or somewhere else in New England.

These guys have such a life carved out for themselves. They have their homes and their history.

They communicate without speaking, half the time. How am I supposed to fit into that?

Do I even want to fit into that?

The shower really does help ease some of my aching and anxiety. The water pressure is amazing, and the temperature is just right, nice and hot to ease my aching muscles. There's a tiny part of me that takes note of how big the shower is—it's insanely huge—and wants to ask the men if they'd like to join me.

Warm water and three handsome, muscled bodies? It's a perfect, and tempting, combination.

No, Kiara, for fuck's sake, I tell myself sternly. My life is in danger, and I need to focus.

And as nice as the shower is, it also gives my mind the chance to race, to second-guess trusting these men. What do I really know about them, after all? Next to nothing. I know their heritage, but that's about it. I don't even know what their jobs are.

Clearly, they're a family. You can see it just in how they interact. But can I trust them when they say that I'm their mate? Really? Sure, they protected me—twice—from bounty hunters, but they took care of those guys easily. It was like watching football players go up against twelve-year-olds. The preteens don't stand a chance.

But what about when the chips are *really* down? When they're put in a position where they might actually be in serious trouble? Will they stick by me then?

Nobody ever has.

You've never given anyone the chance, another part of me speaks up.

That's... true. The closest I've gotten to anyone in years is, or was, Jason, and look at how well that turned out. So can I really expect them to trust me when I'm not trusting them?

Ugh, it's like an awful feedback loop. I glare ahead at the tiles, as if it's a mirror, and I can reflect my own glare back at myself. This is far too complicated. This is not what I signed up for. I signed up for getting my shit together and getting Donovan off my back.

"Thanks for that, universe," I grumble.

"You all good in there? Need any towels?" Cain asks, rapping on the door.

Fuck! I jump a mile. "Yup! All good!"

"You can stay in there as long as you want, we won't run out of hot water," Cain informs me.

"Great, thanks!" I wonder if he can tell I'm hiding from them.

Probably. These men aren't stupid.

I practically hold my breath until I hear Cain walk away, and then I let it out slowly. Okay. This is fine. This is a complication. My feelings are complicated. That's fine. I can handle whatever comes my way. Even if it's these three... mates. Or not mates. I'm still not sold on this mate thing.

I just have to keep my wits about me. I can't let pretty faces distract me. Just because they're loyal to me, or seem to be, doesn't mean they aren't hiding things.

We're going to have to get me some new clothes, too, I realize as I step out of the shower and grab a towel. I've just got the ones I was wearing before. If the guys have a laundry system in here, I can just wash those clothes for tomorrow. That should be fine, but if we end up having to camp out here for a while...

I'm wrapped up in my thoughts about laundry and planning as I step out of the bathroom, still just wrapped in my towel.

But my forward momentum is broken suddenly as I bump into Cain.

We both freeze, the two of us standing in the hallway, staring at each other. I usually don't really care about my state of dress—or undress—but suddenly, I'm painfully aware that I'm just in a towel, my skin still flushed and damp from the water.

Cain's eyes track down my body, and I can see his eyes growing darker as he takes me in. I shiver, heat rising in me. I try to stamp it out, ignore it. I was just worrying about these men. I can't go jumping back into bed with them.

Even though I really, really want to.

"Um." I hold up my clothes. "Do you guys have a way for me to wash these?"

"Yeah, we have a washer and dryer in the closet." Cain pauses. "You'll have to be in that for about an hour, though. Unless... we have some spare clothes lying around."

His voice is rough, a bit strangled, like he's trying hard to hide how much the idea turns him on. And now the idea's turning *me* on—the idea of wearing clothes that are slightly too big for me, that smell like the men—or just lying around in a towel and tempting them—

I don't know which idea is hotter, to be honest.

Cain's staring at me like he's going to devour me. I have got to keep this conversation on track. Or walk away. But I can't seem to get my legs to work. "The—the guy. Back at the market. Magician sorcerer tattoo guy."

Cain raises an eyebrow, looking amused. "Very eloquent."

"Oh, hush." I glare at him. It's his fault I'm stumbling over my words. And he knows it. "You all knew him."

"Yes. We'd gotten help from him before with some small magical issues. His specialty is concealment." Cain looks away, and I swear I can see fire sparking in his eyes, actual demonic fire, like he's imagining setting the man ablaze and is wishing he hadn't let him live.

"We used him for a few jobs in the past. Just little things. We needed an invisibility spell added to a jacket, that kind of thing. Nothing major. We like to test people out with a few smaller jobs before we trust them with anything really big. So far he'd been legit." Cain's lip curls up. "But I guess the lure of the reward was too much.

"It's our fault. We should've shown him how powerful we were from the start. We like it when people underestimate us, but if he'd been properly afraid of us then he never would've dared try to betray us and turn you in." Cain looks back at me. "I'm sorry."

"It's not your fault," I point out. "You can't read minds and you only met me yesterday. How were you supposed to plan for something that you didn't even know was going to happen? You were being smart and protecting yourself. You can't blame yourself for that."

Cain gives a small smile. "Thank you. You're gracious."

"I'm kind of the opposite of gracious," I point out. "Look, I get that you're convinced I'm your fated mate. But I don't want you thinking that I'm better than I am. I don't want to... to disappoint you."

After all, if their expectations are low, then I don't have to worry about letting them down.

"Aww, you worried about your reputation?" Cain teases me. He reaches up and moves some of my still-damp hair back behind my shoulder. He's not touching me, but I can feel the warmth of his hand.

It takes a lot not to shiver in response. It's hard to hide how easily these men turn me on.

"I don't have a reputation to worry about," I shoot back.

Cain's fingers trail along my shoulder, and I swallow. Cain grins. "You can admit you want me." He winks.

"Who says I want that?"

"I want you," he says bluntly. "We all do. All the time."

"How can you just admit that?" I blurt out. "It gives me power over you."

"Maybe," Cain acknowledges. "But not as much as you might think. There are other ways for people to have power over you. You're our mate, which means why should we bother hiding how we feel? We want you and besides..." He smirks. "There's a lot of fun that we can get up to."

I suppose I get what he's saying, but if I admit how much I'm attracted to these men, it could mean that they're right about the fated mates business. Or at least,

SADIE MOSS

they'll think that they're right. And they could think that I'll do what they want just because I want to have sex with them.

"How did you know that he was going to betray us?" I ask, desperate to get us back into safer territory. "How did you know he would... try to bind me or hurt me?"

When the guy first grabbed me, I'd thought he was trying to yank me out of the way or help me. How did Cain know when I didn't?

"I don't trust anyone," Cain replies. "I just assume everyone will betray us."

"I shouldn't have let my guard down," I admit. "I try not to trust people, but then I just let this random magician do whatever. I shouldn't have..."

"Hey." Cain puts a hand on my arm. I light up all over. "That's what we're here for."

"Are you saying you trust me?" I ask.

Cain shakes his head, a small smile tugging at the corners of his mouth. "No. I only trust North and Raven. No one else."

His eyes are still filled with heat, though.

I swallow. I could ignore that heat. I probably should. I feel like I'm in a dance, playing a game where we're competing against each other. "You want to sleep with me but not trust me?"

"Oh, and you trust me, do you?" Cain points out, his

fingertips brushing against my towel. Like he's considering ripping it off of me.

Heat crawls up my spine. He's distracting me, or so the warning voice in the back of my brain says. But I kind of want to be distracted. I want to make this... playful. Because we're getting into dangerous territory. I don't want to spill my secrets.

"Maybe I do, maybe I don't," I reply. "I'm not the one who's sold on the whole mate thing. It's your job to convince me, remember?"

"Oh, it's my job, is it?" Cain chuckles. He sounds incredibly amused by me.

Normally I'd feel condescended to, but I don't feel that way with Cain. It feels more like I'm a poisonous snake and he knows it in how he's handling me, as he's trying to be careful with me. But I suspect he just meets everything in life with humor.

"Well, I'm not going to just fall swooning into your arms like a heroine in an old movie," I point out. "You've got to work for that."

"Oh, I don't think you're the swooning type of girl at all," Cain agrees, very seriously. He eyes me up and down and it feels like the heat from him, his demonic nature, is landing on my skin, warming me up in turn. "None of us expect you to buy into this right away, Kiara." He pauses. "Except maybe Raven. But you're allowed to have some concerns. That's why we'll prove to you that we're worthy mates."

"But you just said you don't trust me."

"And I don't." A bit of an edge enters Cain's voice.

"But why not?" I ask. I'm teasing him a little, and I really shouldn't. Not when I'm a hypocrite for not trusting them. "I'm your mate."

Cain inhales sharply, and then takes a step into me so that I'm pinned against the doorframe, trapped between solid wood and his body. His fingertips trail down my jaw, my throat, then lower. I whimper.

"I don't have to trust someone to protect them," Cain points out. He tilts my chin up, and a moment later I feel his tongue lap against my skin, tasting a stray water droplet that slides down my neck. "Or to sleep with them."

His voice is pure sex, and I squirm helplessly. I've never been so powerless to my own lust before. I've never wanted anyone as much as I do these three men. It's intoxicating, but also fucking terrifying. What the hell is happening to me? I've never let my distrust of people be overwhelmed by my desire before. But I just *want* so badly—

I'm not sure which one of us moves, Cain or me, but the next thing I know, we're kissing.

He's so good at it, teasing, drawing me out until I'm

moaning with it, desperate. His thigh shoves between mine, and I grind down, grabbing onto his arms, sucking on his tongue. Sparks are flying inside me.

For a second, I'll be honest, I think I've orgasmed. What else could this pure white feeling in my eyes be? But then I realize... it's not an orgasm. I know what those feel like, the rushing pleasure of them, and this isn't pleasure. Not really.

Everything clears, and it strikes me in a rush what this is.

It's a vision.

My very first.

CHAPTER 11

F ae all supposedly have the Sight, the ability to see things that aren't right in front of us. It's what Raven and Cain just did on the couch, to locate the Aurora Gem.

Some people say that all fae are connected, that we're all just pieces of one great... spirit? Soul? Thing. Others say that you can see what will be or what was. Not just the present in other places, but the future and the past.

But I've never had the Sight. If I did have it, I'd be able to try to use it to find an Aurora Gem myself. I think part of it is that I lost my parents when I was young. I never had anyone to teach me. I've been operating as a human this whole time.

Sometimes, I wondered if it was just me. If I was... not enough, as a fae. If I was weak. I was trying to be human anyway, though, so what the hell did it matter, right?

But now, I'm definitely seeing something.

I feel like I'm not even in my body. Or rather... like I'm not connected to it. I'm seeing through a body, but I can't feel it or control anything. I can only see. I think I'm floating?

Right up ahead of me stands a woman. She looks—a lot like me, actually. Tall, light brown skin, thick brown hair, an Amazon's build. Snapping dark eyes. But she has this air of power and command that I've never had. This woman looks like the epitome of confidence and royalty.

Yeah. She looks... regal.

Of course, all of this could have something to do with the fact that she's leading a whole damn army of fae.

My jaw would drop if it could do that right now. This army is huge. It's clearly an important battle.

Is that me? Am I doing that? She looks just like me. I don't see how it could be anyone else. But it can't possibly be me. I'm a loner, I work by myself. I've never led anyone in my life.

Everything shifts, like looking through a kaleidoscope, and next thing I know I'm *in* the woman. We're the same person. I'm still not in charge, I can't control anything. It's just a new perspective.

The two of us—or rather, me in this woman's body, or her with me as a ride-along, it's hard to tell—stand strong and raise our arm up into the air, and everyone seems to cheer in response. I can't hear anything, for some reason. I can only see. But people are opening their mouths and seem to be cheering.

Am I saying something? I can't tell if our mouth is moving or not. But people are reacting as if they've just heard a rousing, inspiring speech. Everyone's wearing armor, including me. But I can't see our enemy. I can't even see where exactly we are. Are we in the middle of a field? In a city? This army of mine seems to be just on the bare ground with nothing but a vague background, like someone was doing a painting and hasn't finished yet. There's just blank canvas all around.

I'm standing above everyone, I realize. I'm either on some kind of platform or raised hill, something that puts me higher than everyone else. Or maybe it's not literal but metaphorical. People looking up to me, viewing me as their leader, and having all this power. I don't know what to do with it.

This person does though. Or this version of me. I can

feel her. She's got no room for questions. She's doing what she has to do with confidence. Not confidence that she'll win, but confidence that she's doing the right thing. That this is what's necessary, and she's going to give every single bit of herself to it.

That level of dedication, of grit and strength, is inspiring. No wonder these people are cheering for her. Could I ever be like that? Could I ever be someone that people look up to? That feels a part of something, maybe even a leader of it, instead of alone and on the outside?

For some reason, my mind notices that she's alone. Or I'm alone. We're alone. There's not three men around her. She's all by herself. Even though she's a part of something, she's not one of the crowd, she's not standing shoulder to shoulder with comrades. She's just herself. Still alone, just in a different way.

That hurts a little.

Maybe this means I won't end up with these men. Maybe this whole fated mate thing isn't real or won't take, or something.

The other possible option is that the men are dead, and for some reason that makes me feel a horrible, aching sadness need inside me. Maybe that's why she's fighting. Maybe it's to avenge them. But that idea feels wrong. Not wrong like incorrect, but wrong like it hurts.

Something shifts again and suddenly I can feel my

body again. My eyes are opening even as I start to realize they were closed. I stare up around me.

I'm lying on the couch, still in the towel, the three men hovering over me. Cain's squinting, looking curious and analytical. Raven's eyes are wide with worry. North looks confused.

"Kiara?" North asks. "You all right?"

I nod, wincing a little. "I... I'm sorry about that."

For some reason, I want to smile. I just feel so happy staring up at the men. Like something is settling deep inside me, content. If I was a cat, I'd be purring.

"You know, I've been told I'm good at sex," Cain jokes, "but I've never made someone pass out before."

"I didn't pass out. Not exactly." I sit up slowly.

Raven immediately hands me a glass of water. I smile at him gratefully and he blushes.

"I had a vision," I explain, taking sips of water. The urge to cuddle close to the men is overwhelming. I just... I feel safe with them. "I've never had one before."

North's face grows a bit... shuttered. "You never had it until now?"

I shake my head.

North nods, patting my shoulder. He seems sympathetic. "Raven, Cain, you two have got this."

He kisses the top of my head and then stands and

goes into the kitchen, rooting around in the cupboards. It doesn't look like he's actually trying to do anything. More like he's just trying to distract himself. His jaw is clenched, and his back and shoulders are drawn together, hunched.

Is North upset?

"Did I do something wrong?" I ask, looking over at the other two.

Cain shakes his head, smiling. Raven puts a hand on my knee. "No, never. You couldn't do anything wrong."

I raise an eyebrow at him. Cain chuckles.

"So this was your first vision, huh?" he asks me. "How do you feel?"

"Um... exposed."

"That would be the towel."

"Very funny. No, I mean..." I shake my head. "Vulnerable. Like I need to feel safe." I don't know how to say that the three of them make me feel safe. "Like when you're in the shower and somebody rips open the curtain."

Cain nods. "It does feel like that, yes. Especially when you're looking at your own past or future instead of seeing something from the present. Or someone else's past or whatever."

Raven also nods, in agreement.

"The more you do it, the more used to it you'll get," Cain assures me. "It's just like anything else, practice makes perfect. If you'll excuse the metaphor..." He winks. "It's almost like having sex for the first time. When you first have sex you're so overwhelmed, it's all too much. And you can't really control yourself or be very good at it. But the more you do it the better you get at it, and it still feels good, but it doesn't overwhelm you. Make sense?"

"Yeah, that makes sense." I finish off my water. Raven takes it and sets it aside. "Were you guys able to make any progress on research?"

The two men look at each other sheepishly. "We were looking after you," Cain says. "You were out for an hour and a half."

"What?" It doesn't feel like I was out for that long. How did that happen? The vision felt like it was only a minute.

Cain nods. "Yup. Visions never feel as long as they really are. When Raven and I were searching earlier for the gem, it felt like only a few seconds."

"And you three didn't... do anything during that time?"

"How could we? We had to keep an eye on you and make sure you're okay," Raven says. He sounds completely serious, as if it never even occurred to him or the others to do anything other than look at me and keep an eye on me.

Wow. It feels almost like I've been hit by a truck. These three really are devoted to me.

What am I supposed to do with that?

CHAPTER 12

We spend the rest of the day doing research, trying to find where this Aurora Gem would be based on the building Raven and Cain saw.

I can't help but watch the men interacting with each other. They look like they're the same age that I am, maybe a couple years older, in their mid-twenties. But their behavior reminds me that they're so much more. There's a familiarity between them, and a confidence, that is so much deeper than their apparent ages.

And they care about each other. Raven makes us all sandwiches, and he doesn't even have to ask North and Cain what they prefer. He just knows already. North and Cain smile at him as Raven sets the food down and pats them on their shoulders. They're very tactile with each other—Cain ruffles Raven and North's hair even though the two playfully scowl at him. North constantly nudges the others, like a dog bumping up against its owners' legs.

Such casual, easy affection. I've never had that before. Watching them do it is... it fills me with yearning, actually. Jason was never like this with me. Partly because I kept him at arm's length.

The men aren't touching me like that, but that's probably more because I'm keeping myself at a distance. Would they touch me like this if I let them? Would they let me touch them in return, really make me a part of their family?

I could be a part of this. Theoretically. But... should I? Can I really? What if I take it and then it's ripped away from me, the same as my parents were? What if they just want me to be some pretty prize, their fragile mate to protect and not really a proper part of the family?

You're being paranoid, I tell myself. *Calm the fuck down.*

Raven sets my own sandwich down in front of me. "Thanks," I tell him.

Raven smiles, pleased. He's so quiet, but his devotion is the most obvious. I don't know what to do with it. Should I... talk to him about it? Reach out and touch him?

"I think I've found where we need to go," Cain says. He turns his laptop screen to show us. "This is the building that we saw. It's in Nevada."

"Nevada?" I lean in. That doesn't look like a building so much as a ruin. An old abandoned fort from the days of the Wild West.

"Found it on a history site," Cain explains. "Apparently it's the remains of some old supernatural settlement from when we were taming the west or whatever. Humans don't really know about it. I couldn't find a whole lot of information, but I bet you it's haunted."

"Things aren't haunted." North rolls his eyes.

"You're half shifter and half fae, and you refuse to believe in ghosts?"

This sounds like an old argument between them.

"You show me proof of ghosts—"

"I shouldn't have to show you proof—"

"And I'll believe it, we have documented cases of other supernaturals, I can run into a vampire or a werewolf or a troll in the street any day. And you expect me to believe in a ghost when in all my years I've never seen—"

"They don't *want* you to see them that's the whole *point*—"

"Guys." I snap my fingers. "Building. Nevada. Why

would the Aurora Gem be in this rundown pit of all places?"

Cain's eyes go white again for a couple minutes as he uses his Sight. When he comes out of it, Raven passes him a glass of water, the same as he did with me. Raven doesn't talk much, so I'm guessing that this is how he shows his affection for people—through physical acts of service and caring.

"There's a huge network of caves beneath it," Cain says. "The gem must be hidden in there somewhere."

Aurora Gems are extremely powerful, so those that own them tend to hide them away so that they don't get into the wrong hands. Of course, whose hands are the wrong hands are up for debate, and I don't really care too much about adding to that debate. Highest bidder is all that works for me.

"Do we have any idea who owns it?" I ask. "Who put it there?"

"No idea." Cain shakes his head.

"We don't want to piss off someone else," North points out.

"This place looks like it hasn't been disturbed in years," Cain replies. "I think that whoever put it there originally forgot about it. Or they died."

"It wouldn't be the first time someone tried to have

something vulnerable hidden away and then died and never got to use it," I point out.

"Fair," North accepts. "But we know a thing or two about sticking something valuable out in the middle of nowhere. Doesn't mean that there isn't some kind of alert if we try to break in."

That makes me curious. Do they have something valuable hidden in the middle of nowhere with protections on it and an alert that they'll hear if someone tries to go in? The thief in me is fascinated by the possibility and wants to know more, but I keep my thoughts to myself.

"I think that's a chance we'll have to take," I admit. "Someone could be keeping an eye on this gem but they also could've died. It happens a lot. It's a question of are we willing to risk the odds?"

"I am," Cain says.

Raven nods. But both men look at North.

North nods as well.

"Okay. So we go there and get the gem out. Any idea what kind of traps or alarm systems we'll be dealing with going in?" I like to do reconnaissance before I do a job. It's what any burglar does, you have to know the ins and outs, the potential pitfalls. I couldn't just waltz into a joint and wing it. I had to do my homework.

"No." Cain shakes his head and sips his water. "I

didn't see enough, just a glimpse to know there are tunnels."

"We can assume there are traps," North goes on. "Places like these always have them."

He says it with such casual confidence, as though he's dealt with all of these things before—not just once but enough times that it's routine, nothing to worry about. I wonder what sort of lives these three have led, that they're so ready to go with this, that they've got a safe house, that breaking into a system of caves that are probably—definitely—rigged to get an Aurora Gem of all things isn't that big of a deal.

I swallow my questions. If I ask them questions, they'll start asking me questions, and I'm curious, but I don't know if I can reciprocate. I don't know if I can answer whatever it is they might ask me. I don't know if I can give myself away just yet.

"Okay. If you guys think that we can handle this, then I'm trusting you on that." They seem like capable fighters, judging by the market fight. "But I'm the burglar here, so unless you three are used to breaking into places and detecting traps, we'll be following my lead when we get in there."

Cain and Raven look at North.

North thinks about it for a second, then nods at me. "We'll trust you on this. You're the expert."

I don't know too much about shifters, but North practically oozes alpha male, and the other two look to him for leadership. "Thank you," I tell him. It has to mean a lot for him to agree to defer to my expertise.

"We'll set out in the morning," North says, standing. "We want to give Donovan's men time to lose the trail and run around in circles. Lose track of us."

I could probably use the rest. I know I was technically lying on the couch during my vision but it didn't feel like I was. Between that, the fight, and everything else, I'm exhausted. And nervous.

"We'll need some supplies," North adds. "I'll go out and get a few things. Cain, with me. Raven, you're on guard."

Cain stands, and Raven nods, both of them immediately following orders. North doesn't growl or snap to show his authority. He doesn't have to.

"Be careful," Raven warns them fondly as the other two head out. Raven's the worrier, I'm starting to realize.

He doesn't look like he would be. He's huge, covered in tattoos, he looks like he doesn't need to ever worry about anything.

Cain kisses me on the top of my head, then follows North out of the safe house. I can't even see the front door—it's like they just open a portion of the wall and then vanish.

Raven cleans everything up. I'm not quite sure what to do—I don't have pajamas, and I don't want to wear my normal clothes to sleep in, so I start going through the closets to find something to wear.

"Do you guys mind if I borrow some clothes?" I ask.

"No, not at all." Raven seems unsure what to do now that it's just the two of us. I feel like he's a dog on a leash, being held back, but not in a scary way. Not like he's going to attack me. More like he just wants to come to me and be close, and he doesn't know how.

I find a pair of shorts and a t-shirt, I think one of Cain's, and I go to change in the bathroom.

Raven's still sitting there when I come back. He looks lost.

"Do you want to do anything?" I ask. "Play a card game?"

I'm joking, but Raven looks up at me, dead serious. "Do you want to? We can do that. We can watch TV or we can talk."

I have a feeling that if I told him I wanted him to talk, he'd just start talking nonstop, to please me. That... concerns me. I don't want anyone to be so devoted to me that they were giving up their own autonomy. I don't want a slave.

"No. I want to know what you want to do."

That seems to throw Raven for a loop. For a second,

a look of worry crosses his face, like he's thinking he's done something wrong.

"I want you to do what you want," I clarify. "Not what I want. If you want to do something, and I want to do the same thing then great, but you aren't—I don't know about this mate thing. I don't know how it works. But I'm pretty sure that it doesn't mean you have to sacrifice your own choices and your own wants for mine."

Raven seems to take this in, then tilts his head at me. He's staring at me in a way that heats me up all over. I can practically see him thinking about what he wants, and I swallow at the implications of the heat in his gaze. It's pretty obvious how he wants us to spend the time.

"Do you mean that?" He stands up and walks over to me. "Do you really want me to do what I want?"

I have a feeling I know where this is going. Raven's staring at me like he wants to devour me, and I can feel my knees going weak. Raven's huge, and gorgeous, and I can't help but remember the night I had with the three of them.

Raven reaches me, putting his hands on my hips. His breath shudders out almost like he's scared of how much he wants this.

I'll be honest, I'm scared too of how much I want this. I want what we had the other night. I want Raven to touch me again, kiss me again, and I know that he can read my expression and tell that I want it too.

"Yes," I tell him. And I mean it, more than I've ever meant anything.

As if that single word is all he's been waiting to hear, Raven pulls me in by the hips and kisses me.

Oh, fuck, yes.

All three men kiss so differently. Raven's intense but thorough, deliberate, like he's going to take me apart slowly, piece by piece, until I'm a complete wreck. His hands ground me, and I slide my own hands over his arms, feeling the muscles, knowing his tattoos are under my fingers, sliding beneath the pads like ink.

I should probably stop and keep my level head. I can't keep sleeping with these men when I don't know if I want them as my mates or not—or if I even want a mate at all. But fuck, he kisses so well. I feel like I'm slowly melting, bit by bit, not a boiling heat but a simmering one.

Raven's hands slide down to my thighs, lifting me up, and I squeak in surprise—I don't squeak. He carries me the few steps across to the large bed, lying me down on the bed, my legs spread as he settles between them. His body is so heavy and broad on top of mine, it sends a delicious thrill through me. I love it.

I wrap my legs around him, uncaring in the moment

about whether this is right or wrong, about whether this is the smart thing to do. Raven's practically vibrating, and the idea that someone needs me that much, wants me that much? It's such a turn on.

I've never had anyone be so open in their desire for me. It's intoxicating.

We keep kissing, I have no idea for how long, and I can feel Raven's cock hardening against me. Fuck, yes. I know that I should put a stop to this, but I want it so badly, I want Raven so intensely that I can't think straight. His hands are sliding up underneath my clothes, tugging on my hair, he's kissing down my neck...

Then the front door opens.

Raven leaps to his feet, snarling as he transforms into his gargoyle form, clearly ready to fight whoever he has to in order to protect me.

"Just us," Cain says cheerfully, striding in behind North and closing the door.

Awkwardness falls.

North and Cain both tilt their heads, staring hungrily at the two of us as they realize what they interrupted. Raven shifts back to his more human form, glancing back and forth between all of us, clearly a bit embarrassed.

I have no idea what to think or feel, how to handle this. Part of me is still buzzing with desire and energy.

But I can't do this. I'm trying to keep my head above water with Donovan, and I still don't know about this mate business. I can't toy with their hearts like this.

"Um." I sit up and adjust my clothes. "I'm going to, uh, go brush my teeth. Get ready for bed."

Feeling like a coward, I scurry into the bathroom and shut the door. Bracing my hands on the sink, I try to calm myself down with several deep breaths.

Clearly, my desire for them is overriding my common sense. That's never happened to me before. It's great in some ways but absolutely terrifying in others. My whole life I've only been able to rely on myself and my judgment. I've never trusted anyone. How can I handle myself if I'm compromised by my desire for these men?

I still have no idea what to say when I exit the bathroom again, but I have to deal with this. This isn't a huge safe house, after all.

I don't see North, but Cain and Raven are doing some kind of... thing against the wall. A door opens, as if they've just created it. Cain looks over his shoulder and sees me.

"We thought you might want a room of your own," he explains.

Raven looks sheepish.

I want to tell Raven that this isn't his fault that I'm...

fucked up. But I don't know what to say. "Thanks. I, uh, hope you two sleep well."

"Of course." Cain bows elaborately, clearly doing it on purpose, and gestures for me to enter the room.

It's a small room, and I realize that it's actually a panic room that the two men have modified to be a bedroom for the evening. They must've been hard at work with the magic and supplies while I was panicking in the bathroom.

Clever of them, actually, to have an additional panic room. Nobody thinks, once they've found the safe house, that there could possibly be yet another hiding space inside. Because they think they've already found it.

There's a rather comfy-looking bed, and I crawl right into it. I have to be well rested for tomorrow, and after the crazy last twenty-four hours I've had, I could use some good sleep.

Raven steps forward. Cain's looking at him like he was nudging Raven to do this while I was in the bathroom. "Kiara, I just want you to know... What I want is to be close to you. And to help you be happy."

That's really sweet. I'm still a little concerned about his level of devotion to me. But the idea that it's all he wants, just to be close to me and make sure I'm happy, is possibly the most selfless thing I've ever heard from anyone. Isn't that what you're supposed to feel when you're in a relationship with someone? To want their happiness and to just spend time with them?

"Thank you," I tell him. I should probably say more but how do I even begin to articulate all the confusing emotions that I'm feeling? I'm grateful, but also intimidated by such utter devotion.

"Goodnight," I say, feeling like a coward.

Cain and Raven don't seem upset. "Goodnight, Kiara."

They close the door, separating us.

CHAPTER 13

I lie in bed for hours, but sleep doesn't come.

I can't stop thinking about everything that's happened. I caught my boyfriend cheating, I had the most amazing sex of my life with three supernatural men after spending years only being with humans, and now those men are apparently my fated mates? Then Donovan's men attacked twice, and now I'm in a safe house in an abandoned subway line so that I can go to Nevada of all places, with these mates, to get an Aurora Gem and hopefully get Donovan off my back.

Absolutely nuts.

And if I'm this attracted to them just in one day of knowing them, enough to override my judgment, how bad will it be the more time I spend with them?

I toss and turn. The bed's comfy, but it feels a bit big

and empty after spending the night before with three warm, strong bodies around me, holding me. I'd felt so safe with them and looked after, it had been easy to fall asleep. I feel exposed right now. Vulnerable.

How is it that in just one day I've come to dislike being alone? Or is it more that I disliked being alone this whole time, and I never realized it until now with these men in my life, all of them so eager to be with me?

Or, well, some of them more eager than others. I remember what Cain said. *I don't trust anyone.* He said he didn't have to trust me to care about me or protect me. I don't get that. How can you love someone if you don't trust them? Doesn't that mean you'll always be holding them at arms' length?

And where does North stand on all of this? He hasn't said anything about his thoughts on me. Raven's openly devoted and Cain is at least honest with me about his feelings but North is just there. Quiet.

As if I've summoned him with my thoughts, the door opens, and North pokes his head in, checking on me. I'm not sure where he was earlier, but he still seems a bit tense now.

I sit up. "Is something wrong?"

He steps inside, closing the door after him. "No, everything's fine." He walks over and sits on the edge of the bed, moving with grace and confidence—like a wolf through a forest. "Sorry. I didn't mean to wake you. Just wanted to check in."

"I wasn't asleep."

"You need to rest."

"I can't." I shrug, feeling a bit exposed, vulnerable. "Too many thoughts going on in my head."

North reaches out, running his fingers lightly through my hair, cupping my cheek and brushing his thumb back and forth across my skin. "I could help you... relax."

My breath hitches. His voice is full of promise. Not just about sex, but about the implication that he's taking care of me. That this is just another way to make sure I'm happy.

Part of me wants to give in, but I really know that I shouldn't. And another part of me just wants to blurt out everything that I'm feeling, all the emotions I'm struggling with.

Maybe I'm a coward, but I don't talk about either of those things. Instead I deflect with some humor.

"Hilarious." I push his hand away. "Sleeping pills would probably be more helpful, thanks."

North doesn't move. I have a feeling it takes a lot to intimidate this guy. "Why can't you sleep? What's on your mind?"

I sigh. "Just the world outside the safe house. I've

had a concealment charm on me this whole time and it was like—I don't think I realized what a security blanket it was until it was gone. Now there's no guarantee that I'll be safe outside this house." I pause. "There's no guarantee that you three will be safe, either."

North looks pleased at that, pleased that I'm worried for him and the other two men. Then his face grows serious again.

"You don't have to worry about us. We can take care of ourselves." He pauses, then grimaces slightly. His voice dips down, going quiet. "We... do what we can, anyway."

This is the first time that I've heard him sound anything but confident. He sounds upset, almost. But not at me.

"Would you like to shift?" I ask. "I don't mind."

Shifters sometimes feel more comfortable in their animal form than in their non-animal form. He doesn't have to hide his wolf from me. I won't be upset.

"No."

His tone startles me. "Aww, what, you don't want to show me your big bad wolf?" I tease him. I'd actually kind of love to see his wolf—petting one sounds like a great idea right about now, very soothing.

North, to my surprise, gets even sharper in his tone. "No," he practically snaps.

"Oh. I'm." Uh. This is awkward. "I'm sorry."

This is... spoiled of me, probably, but I'm confused. This is the first time since meeting them that one of these three has denied me anything, and he sounds like the Beast from *Beauty and the Beast* when Belle asks what's in the West Wing. Is there a shifter custom I don't know about that I've violated? Have I hurt him somehow? It seems odd that this of all things would be what he denies me after the men have made a big point about my being their mate.

North goes stiff, but nods, as if he accepts my apology. He looks about as awkward as I now feel. He gets up. "I'll see you in the morning."

Okay then.

North leaves, closing the door behind him, and I lie back down, confused. What—what am I supposed to do with these men? What made North so upset? And why do I even care? I've never wanted to know about anyone before. They kept to their business, and I kept to mine. So what if there were questions or awkwardness? It wasn't my business.

But I do want to know. I want to know why North was awkward, why he said no, what he's feeling.

I've never cared about anyone else before. And now that I do... it scares me.

It takes me a long time to fall asleep.

CHAPTER 14

We take a portal to Nevada, but that's only going to buy us so much time before whatever bounty hunters are after me will catch up to us. If you could shake off bounty hunters or mob collectors simply by taking a portal, then everyone would do it, and nobody with a bounty on their heads would ever get caught.

But taking a portal will buy us a bit of time, and it's the only way to really get to Nevada in any timely fashion.

We arrive in Las Vegas, which is kind of my paradise. I would love to rob this place blind. The human places, anyway. There are some supernatural-owned casinos, and they've got more security than the

White House. You don't break into one of those unless you've got some kind of death wish, and I do not have one of those, thanks. I stay far away from supernatural casinos.

But there's no time for me to indulge my desire to play *Ocean's Eleven* at The Luxor. We rent a car and head straight out into the desert, toward the building that Cain and Raven saw.

It's way out in the middle of nowhere, away from civilization, and we spend some time in the car together. Raven's driving again. North is sitting in the front this time, though. I wonder—is he upset about last night, still? Did I say something wrong? Hurt his feelings in some way?

Normally I don't care about that kind of thing. It feels... disconcerting to care so much about it now.

Cain sits with me, occasionally leaning forward to murmur to Raven as they make sure they're heading in the right direction based on their visions. He smiles at me encouragingly, and winks.

"Don't you worry about a thing, sweetheart," he tells me. "Raven and I know what we're doing."

Normally I would bristle at anyone calling me 'sweetheart'. But Cain sounds like he really, truly means it—like he thinks I have a sweet heart.

I don't know what to do with that, or the warm feeling that it causes in my chest.

We travel down dirt highways that I think the rest of humanity—and time—has forgotten, until we reach a set of absolute ruins. I think there might be some kind of magical shielding charm still in place around the building, because one moment it's not there, the next it is, rising up out of the hard-packed desert earth.

Raven parks the car and we stare up at the ruins. It really does look rundown, the sort of place that's definitely haunted in movies.

"Looks just like the vision," Cain murmurs.

I'm impressed in spite of myself. I've never seen any fae use the Sight before, so I have to admit I wondered about how accurate it was. How much guesswork is involved and how much of it is just... knowing.

"Looks cheerful," North says dryly.

How much of my own vision was accurate? Was any of it real? A true glimpse in the future, or the past?

I'm tempted to ask Cain and Raven about it, but I don't. I've always kept things close to the vest, and that's a habit that's hard to let go of. Besides, given North's behavior last night, they've clearly got some issues of their own that they're not sharing with me. Why should I share with them?

I'm not quite sure I even want to know if the vision is true.

We all get out of the car, into the heat, which none of us like. Fae get cold easily, it's true, but we're suited for more temperate climates, not this stupid relentless heat. Ugh.

"We should scope it out first," I say. That's always what you have to do when robbing a place, even if you've done reconnaissance before, or research. You can never be too careful.

The men nod without complaint and we inspect the area around the ruins. There don't seem to be any powerful magical wards or security features. Maybe there were, at some point, and they've just expired. Who knows? I can detect a kind of glamour on the ground, though—must've been the reason we couldn't see the building until we were almost right on top of it.

"Anything?" I call out, the other three scattered around the area, inspecting.

"Nothing," Cain calls back to confirm as North shakes his head.

We reconvene in front of what seems to be the main entrance. It's hard to tell, with so much of the place caved in. It looks less like some kind of Wild West fort and more like a castle that someone gave up halfway through building.

Here goes nothing.

I feel along the walls of the entryway as I start to step through, but I don't feel any mechanisms that will activate. That's good, at least. I get inside, and I feel the men fanning out behind me.

Once inside, my jaw drops a little.

This place is much bigger than it looks on the outside. Maybe I should've expected that—it's a supernatural building, after all, one built by our people. Those rarely look the same on the inside as they do on the outside. The ceiling's much higher, and the walls are farther back.

Everything is dimly lit, mostly from the holes in the roof and walls, the sunlight streaming in wherever it can. I squint, trying to look around and see more. There's nothing on the walls, no murals or words. No furniture. Whoever was last in here cleaned this place out, scrubbed it down. Interesting.

"This place wasn't just abandoned," I announce.

"What makes you say that?" Cain asks as Raven looks around, sniffing a little like this place is giving him allergies.

"Abandoned places just have shit lying around. You can't take everything with you." I gesture around us. "There'd be furniture, or knickknacks. You can't take everything with you no matter how much you might want to. This place looks... neat. Like a shell."

"She's right," North agrees, coming up to stand beside me and look around. "This feels deliberate. Someone did this."

"If there's an Aurora Gem here then it was probably done after this place was originally abandoned," I add. "To put in modifications when they hid it."

"What kind of modifications?" Cain asks.

"Security measures, usually. Like traps."

"I don't detect any traps," Cain replies.

Famous last words. A large rumbling noise fills the massive chamber, and huge Indiana-Jones-style boulders appear out of goddamn nowhere.

Fuck.

I quickly phase out as a boulder comes crashing toward me, rolling across the floor like a gigantic marble, and I pass right through it, safe. Cain and Raven are doing the same, but North...

"Why aren't you phasing?" I yell, panic clawing at my throat. I don't want him to get crushed!

North ignores me and instead, as another boulder rolls toward us, jumps up into the air, smacking his palm against the side of the boulder and using it as leverage to leap over it, landing on top.

He leaps onto the next boulder, and the next one, his

momentum keeping him going, heading toward where the boulders seem to be coming from.

"There's a stairway!" he yells.

Phasing to get through the boulders, Cain, Raven, and I take off after North, following him across the chamber. I can see it now too, in between the boulders that cross my field of vision—a stairway leading down.

The three of us make it across as North leaps down from a boulder, landing safely in the entrance. The moment we step onto the first stair, the boulders disappear.

Panting, I stare at the now-empty chamber. That was why it was cleared of everything—to give the boulders room to move around. "There's definitely something valuable in here," I announce.

"No shit," North mumbles.

I put my arm on his shoulder. As hot as it was to see him leaping over the boulders, showing how strong and agile he is, it still put my heart in my throat. "You okay?"

North nods. He looks down at my hand on his arm, looking surprised that I'm asking. "You?"

"I'm okay."

"Good," Cain says, "Because those boulders were just the opening act."

He's joking—I can tell by his tone—but my pulse

quickens. Because serious or not—I'm pretty sure he's right.

Nobody just makes one trap and is done with it. You don't have just one spot where your burglar alarm will go off. You need multiple.

Yeah. That was just the opening act.

CHAPTER 15

Raven steps around me so that he's in front, peering down the stairs. I don't know much about gargoyles, but he seems to have no problem seeing in the pitch-dark ahead of us. "Goes down for a while."

Cain steps up right behind Raven, then raises his hand, a fireball appearing between his fingers. He holds it aloft, and now we can all see that the stairs do in fact go down for a while. I can't see where they even out.

North shifts so that he's behind me, putting a hand on my shoulder.

"Shall we?" he rumbles.

The men are surrounding me now, I can't help but notice. They didn't say anything or even look at each other, but by now I've seen the way they are with each other—how comfortable they are, how well they seem to know each other. The way they work as a unit. They don't need to communicate with each other to act out a plan of surrounding me to keep me safe, they'll just do it.

"Let's," I say, responding to North. If I wasn't okay with a little danger, I wouldn't have become a thief.

North squeezes my shoulder reassuringly, and Raven starts to move forward. I follow him and Cain down the steps, North a warm presence at my back.

No axe blades come out of the wall to slice at us, although I do check the walls and the steps every so often to make sure we aren't going to trigger anything. Whoever created the boulders is a magic user, obviously. They must expect whoever tried to get in here would also be a magic user. That means we have to be prepared for anything.

I'm not sure how deep down the stairs go, but it feels like miles. Cain had said that there were huge tunnels reaching all over underneath this building. Are we going to have to go through a huge maze to find this gem? How deep into the earth are we talking, here?

Just when I think I might start to panic a little, the stairs even out, the walls retreat a little, and we're in a hallway. It's not quite big enough for two of us to stand next to each other, but I can breathe a little easier.

"Watch out for pressure plates," I warn Raven, since he's at the front.

Pressure plates are usually used in safes. If you lift an item off of the plate, it'll trigger an alarm unless you put in the right code first. I know of a couple owners who forgot they had pressure plates and activated them, sending security teams to their apartments for no reason.

Raven nods in acknowledgement, and we head down the hallway, moving slowly as Raven and I keep checking to make sure we're not about to activate any booby traps or anything.

We haven't hit any trip wires. I *know* we haven't. I would feel it—but there's absolutely no warning before I hear something whistling through the air. I don't know what it is, I just know that it's bad, and guessing by the boulders, it's headed for us.

I try phasing out, and I can't. I'm stuck. It feels like I'm trying to clench muscles I don't even have, and I grit my teeth. "I can't phase!"

"Neither can I," Cain admits, sounding frustrated.

"Spears!" Raven yells. I can just barely see over his shoulder, hurtling toward us, what look like about a dozen spears.

North grabs me, shoving me behind him as if he'll shield me with his body no matter what the cost—and then Raven transforms. He grows bigger, his skin turns gray and solidifies, his tattoos vanish into his skin, he becomes monstrous...

And he turns to stone.

A gigantic stone gargoyle is now filling the entire hallway, blocking my view of everything beyond him, his wings spread wide. Two seconds later, I hear the clang of spears hitting the stone, then the soft clatter as they all fall to the ground.

My heart skips a beat. Thank fuck for Raven. There's no way I could've avoided those spears. And if he hadn't done that, we all would've been run through for sure.

"How could you do that while we can't phase out?" I ask.

"My gargoyle form is using my different bloodline. It doesn't work like fae phasing does," Raven explains, shifting slightly back so he's not completely made out of stone. His voice is deeper like this, like stones scraping along a riverbed.

"Gargoyles are rare," Cain says. "I don't think whoever created the spell that keeps us from shifting accounted for the idea that someone like him would be in here."

"Let's go," North orders. "Quickly."

I can hear the whistle of more spears flying at us, and I wince as Raven repeatedly has to turn to stone to keep us from getting hit. This hallway seems to go on forever. How many damn spears are there? Are they just vanishing and then reappearing at the end of the hallway again to start all over?

We at last reach a section of the hallway that turns to the right, and we all quickly follow Raven down it. We pause for a moment, all of us waiting with bated breath. All I can hear is my pounding heartbeat echoing in my ears.

No more spears come.

I let out a sigh of relief. Thank fuck that's over.

"What the fuck?" Cain yells, and oh boy, I spoke too soon.

Something is swinging down from the ceiling. No, multiple somethings, all of them about the size of my damn head.

What the actual fuck?

I've had to deal with magical creatures, sometimes, guarding people's goodies. Usually it's just plain old dogs, but sometimes people get creative. Once you know a creature's weaknesses you can exploit them, animals are predictable that way.

But these are... I don't even know what.

Damn it. What the hell are they?

The creatures swoop down, furred and black, squeaking, and I realize that they're bats. Large, magically modified bats. No real bats get this big, and they sure as hell don't try to bite and claw at people.

They dive for us, squeaking and attacking, aiming for our heads where we're most vulnerable.

At least the hallway has widened, probably to give the bats room, so now we have room to fan out and defend ourselves.

North pulls out two wicked-looking knives. They're specialized blades called kukri, I think. They're slightly curved, with well-worn leather handles that conform perfectly to the shape of his hand. The metal of them glints in the light of Cain's fireball, and North leaps up, using one to slice right through the next bat that comes at him, sending it to the ground in a sickening gush of blood.

Holy shit.

I didn't really get to see North fight in the marketplace, and in the apartment when Donovan's men came after me, we were all just out of bed and he didn't have any weapons on him. This, though, this is—it's insane. As someone who's had to fight a lot of her life, I can appreciate someone who fucking knows what he's doing.

And... well, it's hot.

North slices through more bats, and I look around for a weapon. I don't usually carry one on me and my burglar equipment's not gonna be much help.

The hallway lights up, and I hear a *fwoom*, like

someone just poured gasoline on a grill, and I turn in time to see Cain expertly lobbing two more fireballs at some incoming bats, hitting them clean in the middle of their chests.

"Look out!" he yells as we all duck and the bats go careening through the air, their dying shrieks echoing in my ears.

"What the fuck, Cain," North growls. "This whole place smells like a bad barbecue now."

"What did you expect me to do?"

More bats come at us and Raven snatches them out of the air, throwing them onto the ground and crushing them with his fists and feet, both made out of stone. The rest of him looks normal, or near-human, but his arms and legs are stone, pure crushing power.

Stone... huh...

I look around on the ground, and ah-ha! Stones!

There are a couple that are about the size of my fist. I grab them and toss them in the air a couple times, get a feel for them. I'm not a baseball champion, but climbing up buildings and opening safe locks does give you good hand-eye coordination.

A bat comes toward me, and I shift slightly, waiting until it's right in my best line of sight—and I throw the rock hard as I can.

It smacks right into the bat's face and it goes down,

landing on its back on the ground, twitching. Now that's what we call a concussion.

Another bat comes, and I throw the second rock—it hits the bat a little sideways but sends the animal into the wall, where it hits hard and slides down to land unconscious—or dead—on the floor.

North slices through a few more bats, and then pauses.

We all pause.

There are no more bats. No more squeaking or the fluttering of wings. It's perfectly silent except for our own heavy breathing.

"I think we got all of them," North says, putting his knives away.

I look around at all the dead animals on the floor and wince. They were just doing what their instincts told them to do, and I know we had no choice but to protect ourselves but... it still makes me feel a bit sick. Poor creatures. Whoever did this to them, enchanted them to make them huge and aggressive, is definitely on my shit list now.

Not that my shit list is particularly long.

Cain holds his remaining fireball up so that we can continue to see. "Shall we?" he asks, looking at North.

North nods, and Raven leads the way again as we head down this hallway.

It doesn't take us long to reach our destination—I think the bats were the final big defense. The hallway ends with a large, open doorway, with an octagonal chamber beyond.

I hold up a hand and crouch down, feeling the floor of the doorway. Ah-ha, pressure plate. I jam it so that it won't activate.

"You'll want to step over this," I warn, feeling the air up above me to see if there's a... well I call them a 'curtain alarm'. Basically it's like if you hung a curtain down in a doorway, and every time someone stepped through that curtain, making it move, it would trigger an alarm or defense mechanism.

Only in this case the curtain is invisible, kind of incorporeal, and is made of magic.

I've gotten really good at having a light touch to feel the air, sense where it shifts and becomes something... more, and then I can reach up to the top of the doorway to the source and deactivate it. But it seems this person was just counting on the pressure plate, since I don't feel any more magic in the air.

I stand up. "Okay, we're good."

Just to be on the safe side, I step over the pressure plate, demonstrating for the men. They follow, stepping where I stepped. I never teamed up with anyone before on burglary jobs. There were a few reasons for that, number one being that I didn't trust them not to double cross me, but also because I didn't think they would respect my authority, my expertise on the subject.

More than I would like to admit, it's nice to see these men—these expert, trained fighters who can certainly handle themselves—doing as I say without question or complaint. Trusting that I know what's best.

We all look around the chamber. It's a very simple one, nothing on the walls or anything. No crazy decorations or announcements about some god or other.

"Looks like this wasn't a religious place," Cain remarks.

North grunts in agreement.

"I don't see a gem," I point out, looking at the walls. Is there a panel?

Cain and Raven walk toward the left-hand side of the room. "It was in an alcove," Cain says.

Raven puts his hand on the wall to indicate where.

I walk over, feeling around the area. If it's a sliding panel, not a safe, then the button to activate it should be to the side and a little lower.

My fingers feel something, a depression, then a little hook, and I tug it up. My heart is racing. Finally, after all of this time, I'm going to get an Aurora Gem. I can give it to Donovan, and I'll have my debt wiped clean. I'll be free. No more running, no more hiding, no more fear, no...

The wall under Raven's hand slides upward, revealing a small alcove.

"What the fuck?" Cain says, sounding both shocked and deadpan.

The alcove is empty.

CHAPTER 16

My heart sinks all the way down between my feet. I feel sick.

"So much for fae Sight being accurate," I say, perhaps a little snappier than is warranted. It's not like Cain or Raven did this on purpose, especially Raven who's been nothing but accommodating to me from the beginning. The poor guy looks absolutely sick, like he's so disappointed in himself he might throw up.

"We know what we saw," Cain insists, a stubborn and slightly demonic glint in his eye. "There was an Aurora Gem, right here."

"We should've gone right away," North grumbles. "I shouldn't have suggested we wait. This is my fault."

"So, what, we could run into whoever was trying to

take it and be caught in a fight we weren't prepared for?" Cain points out. "No, hey, don't blame yourself."

Raven nods, in agreement with Cain. They're both looking at North with such supportive affection, and my heart gives a painful thump against my ribcage. They really do all care about each other so much. They're such a unit.

I want to be a part of something like that. Can I? Can I let myself?

"Our Sight isn't wrong," Cain continues, looking over at me. "This gem was here. Someone got to it before we did."

"Who?" I ask.

Cain shakes his head. "I don't know."

I could possibly ask him to try to use his Sight, but that knocked him and Raven out for a while, and I don't want to be stuck in this place any longer than we have to be. "Could you locate another gem?"

"That's not how the Sight works," Cain replies. "It's not like a computer search engine, you can't just type in what you want and it'll tell you what you want to know. If you want to see something specific, you have to manually search for it, like going through bookshelves in a library. And Aurora Gems are rare. It'll be hard to find another one."

Yeah, we got lucky with this one. Fuck. "Okay, but there has to be some way to track whoever was here, then, right? We can't find a new gem or really track this one but we can track people."

And we do have a shifter on us...

I look over at North. "Could you shift into your wolf form and track them that way?"

The moment I say it, I know I've put my foot in my mouth. Raven winces and looks away like he's pretending he isn't there. I'm surprised he doesn't phase out or turn into stone to avoid the conversation entirely.

Cain opens his mouth like he's going to say something, that gleam in his eye that he gets when he's about to explain something to me—only to stop and close his mouth again, looking at North.

"We can find a way to track them without doing that," Cain says at last, when the tension's grown so thick I could cut into it with one of North's knives. "Raven's sense of smell is pretty good, and—"

"No," North cuts in. His tone is final. "Kiara's right. Using my wolf form would be the most convenient way. The easiest way."

Cain looks over at Raven, who still looks like he just would rather be anywhere but here. "We could..." Cain tries again, but North cuts him off.

"No. I'll shift."

I swallow. I feel like I've done something wrong, and that I should make this right, but I don't know how I messed up so I don't know how to fix it or what to say. Should I apologize?

North steps back from us all and a look of immense concentration comes over his face. I've never seen people shifting into their animal form before. I've heard all kinds of different stories, but generally I hear that unlike if you're a lycanthrope—someone who got bitten and is now forced to transform every full moon—a shifter's transformation isn't painful. It's very smooth and natural to them.

But that doesn't seem to be happening here with North. He's got his face screwed up, focusing, and it's clear that he's putting a lot of effort into it, but nothing's happening.

"Relax," Cain advises. "Breathe into it."

North opens one eye to shoot Cain a look, but he does take a deep breath and relax. I wouldn't say that all the tension goes out of his shoulders, but a lot of it does. He's clearly trying to take Cain's advice.

And still, nothing happens.

For a long time, there's no change in him at all. Then, for just the briefest second, his shoulders broaden, his limbs extending as claws protrude from his fingertips. His skin darkens, black fur sprouting all over his body. He looks like a sort of humanoid wolf, unlike any shifter I've ever seen before.

And then something seems to snap, and his regular face and body reappear in a rush. It all happened so fast that I could almost convince myself I imagined the whole thing. It was like he got partway through the shift and couldn't complete it.

Oh. My eyes widen. This was what I sensed last night, wasn't it?

"You can't..." I breathe.

North growls, opening his eyes and shaking himself like he just got out of a bath and is trying to get the water off. "It's no fucking use."

Raven and Cain look at each other sadly, but also resignedly. As if they've seen this happen a hundred times before.

I try to think what it would be like to be unable to phase, to be unable to be, well, a fae. I can't imagine. I know that until recently I haven't had the Sight, and I'm not really fae in my behavior—but a lot of that was my choice. I chose to live as much of a human life as possible.

This feels different. Like North is trying to break through a wall and can't.

"This is pointless," North growls. "Let's go."

Cain and Raven follow obediently. North glances over at me, as if he's wondering if I'll follow, too, and I see such pain and frustration in his eyes, it breaks my heart.

I also see shame.

CHAPTER 17

We don't deal with any threats on the way out. The bats are all dead, the spears don't seem to activate if you're going the opposite direction, and same with the boulders. That's a relief, at least.

It's silent as we make our way to the car. Raven actually doesn't get into the driver's seat this time. He takes the front passenger seat instead.

North takes the driver's seat. He glances at Raven, a grateful expression in his eyes, but he doesn't say anything. It reminds me again how well these men know each other. They don't have to speak or ask. They just know what the other one needs and do it. No thanks are even necessary, because they can feel the gratitude from each other.

I settle into the back, unsure what to say, or if I

should even say anything. I think, from the fact that North is now the one driving, that he needs to be in control right now—or at least to feel more in control. Since he couldn't shift.

Was that why he was running over the boulders earlier? I hadn't really thought about it at the time. I'd been too full of adrenaline. Too worried about us all dying. But does that mean North can't phase out, either? I've never heard of a fae who couldn't do that, or a shifter who couldn't shift.

The drive back is still silent. Not even Cain says anything, not making small chatter. Before, when there were periods of silence, it was comfortable. This is anything but.

We head right back to Vegas and drop the car off at the rental place, then book a suite at a hotel. Not one of the most expensive casinos, but one of the lower-priced ones. We want to blend in with the crowds, but we can't afford to be in the middle of everything if something goes down—it would be hard to explain to non-supernatural people, and I don't want anyone to get hurt.

Once in the suite, Cain starts strategizing. "So it'll take some time, but Raven and I can use the Sight again—"

North growls, not even proper words, and stalks off toward the balcony.

I wince.

Raven sighs and starts looking around the rooms, inspecting everything. Cain gives me a sympathetic look. "I know, he doesn't make it easy."

"I don't understand. He should have the power of both his bloodlines, right?"

"Theoretically," Cain acknowledges. "We have the weaknesses of both sides—so iron still makes us icky. It's not like being half-something-else-that-doesn't-hate-iron makes us immune. If I was half vampire, I'd still have to slop on sunblock and use a parasol when going out in the sun."

"So maybe for some reason that's just... amplified in him?" I ask. "Is that what you mean?"

"Yeah. So that now he has all the weaknesses and none of the strengths. We don't really know for certain. Raven thinks that it's just North himself, that he's got some mental block he has to get over." He shrugs. "I'd hoped that... since we found you, our fated mate, things might get easier for him. But so far..."

I know that it's not my fault that he's like this, but I can't stop a strange twisting feeling of guilt in my gut. Like if maybe I would admit that I was their mate and get on with it, give myself over to this idea, North would be able to shift.

That's not how it works, of course, I know that, but... still. I can't control how I feel.

"I'll go and talk to him," I say.

Cain looks dubious, like he might be about to suggest I just leave North to his alone time, but I slip away and out onto the balcony before Cain can say anything.

North is staring out over the strip, his hands gripping the railings, leaning forward almost like he's trying to catch an elusive scent on the wind. I reach out—I want to touch—but I stop myself right before my hand can land on his back.

I'm not sure if I'm allowed. I want to be helpful. I don't want to drive him away further. But it's been so long since I tried to reach out to someone or let them in, to be a—a part of something, really—and I feel so frustrated with myself I could scream. Why can't I just... know how to be a part of a relationship? Why can't I just know how to support someone?

"Um." I take a deep breath and come up to stand next to him, leaning back against the railing, facing inward so I can keep an eye on Cain and Raven. I can't see Raven, and Cain is in the kitchen looking through the room service menu. Clearly both giving us space.

"Look, I'm not really good at this kind of thing," I admit. "The whole 'talking about feelings' shit. I just... I haven't really had anyone in my life to do that with. But you sound like you could use someone to talk to."

North snorts. "There's no point in talking."

"Oh? So you're just going to do the whole brooding out here thing for, what, an hour? Until you've bottled all your feelings up again? That sure sounds healthy."

North glares at me, but his mouth is twitching like he's also amused and is trying to hide it.

I smile at him.

North huffs and looks back out over the street, at the bustling cars, the people hurrying to beat the heat inside one of the air-conditioned casinos where they can forget their worries and lives, forget time itself.

"Has it always been this way?" I gently prod.

"No," North snaps defensively. He swallows, like he's working on his tone. "No. It wasn't. I could shift as a child."

I nod, trying to be encouraging. I feel like we're two people stumbling around in a pitch-dark room, blind, trying to find each other. "You could just do it? Easily?"

North nods. "It was like breathing. I just swapped around. I could be... this. Or a wolf. Didn't matter."

"What happened?" Did someone hurt him, giving him trauma? Did someone curse him? Usually, when we can't access a part of our inherent magical abilities, it's either from birth or because we were cursed somehow.

North shakes his head, showing his sharpened teeth as he growls in frustration. He might not be able to shift, but there are still wolfish things about him. "I don't know. It was a few years ago."

The words seem to be fighting their way out of his chest, and so I try to keep still. If I say the wrong thing, if I even make the wrong move, he might clam up again and stop confiding in me. I hold still and wait, watching him. I owe him patience.

After all, I'd be just as bad if the shoe was on the other foot.

"Ever since then..." North huffs. "Ever since then, I feel like pieces of me are falling away. I'm losing parts of myself."

"I... I know it's not the same, but..." Fuck, he's confiding in me, and I want to try to show him the same thing, I want to try to be vulnerable too. Sort of a quid pro quo. "I denied my fae self for years. I really only used my powers for burglaries. I lived as a human. Hell, I'm enrolled at NYU."

North doesn't say anything, but he watches me carefully, listening to every word I speak as I continue.

"So now, with you guys knowing about mates and using your Sight and all of that, I—I feel like I'm behind the curve. I didn't know about the market or a lot of other things. I didn't even know who Donovan O'Shae was, or that he was so incredibly powerful until it was too late. If I'd been more of a proper fae, I would've known. I feel like I'd be better at all of this."

North looks at me in surprise, as if he can't imagine the idea that I'd ever think badly of myself. "You aren't lesser, Kiara. You have all your powers. You just don't know how to use them."

"How do you know it's not the same for you, then?" My voice comes out fiercer and more challenging than maybe it should, but I don't care. I never got anywhere in this world by being sweet and nice. "You can't have sympathy for me and none for yourself."

"You're just discovering powers you didn't know you had," North counters. "I had this. Then I lost it. It's not the same thing."

I press my lips together, but I don't know how to dispute that. Because he's right, it is different. "That doesn't mean that all this is lost to you forever."

"It might as well be," North huffs. "I get it. You don't want to... admit that I'm... nothing. I don't want to admit it either. But I couldn't phase out with the boulders. I couldn't shift for you, for my *mate,* when you really needed me to. I'm not a shifter or a fae. I'm nothing."

That takes me aback. How can North possibly think he's nothing? I lay my hand on his arm, finally giving into the urge to touch him. He might not be connected to his wolf side—or so he thinks—but I know that shifters really respond to touch. It means a lot to them. They're all very touchy people.

"You're not nothing," I tell him. "That's a load of bullshit, and I'm not going to stand for it. We've been hunted for so long because of those fucking vampires, and so many of us died. We're all so isolated. No wonder none of us know anything about our culture or our powers. And so many of us are only partially fae, North, it's what we had to do to survive! It's just how it happened! If you're one fae among a fuckton of shifters, of course you'll eventually fall for one of them. It's the law of averages. You're not going to leave and try to seek out another fae just to procreate. We're not animals."

I clench my jaw, trying to wrestle my emotions back under control. "What's happening to you isn't your fault, and it doesn't make you nothing. I'm sure there are tons of fae hybrids out there who have similar issues to you." I squeeze his arm. "You're the leader here. Cain and Raven look to you to make decisions. They trust *you*. And the way you took out those bats? And ran across those boulders? You're not nothing, North. I won't hear it."

I don't think I've spoken so much so quickly before in my life. Not voluntarily, anyway. I don't know where this sense of authority is coming from—I just know that I can't let North keep feeling like shit about himself. Not when I see someone who's so much more than he thinks he is.

"Others aren't fucked up like I am," North growls. He shakes off my hand. "It's not the same. They can access their fae heritage. I can't. Just look at Cain and Raven."

"Cain and Raven would walk on hot coals barefoot if you asked them to. You ran over boulders today, North, that's not fucking useless. You've been protecting me and keeping me safe. That's not useless either."

North turns to face me fully, glaring at me. "You think you can just come in here after knowing me for only a few days and decide you know me better than I know myself?"

"Yes," I snap. "I'm your fated mate, right? Doesn't that mean I should know you? Maybe you need an outsider's perspective. Someone who isn't blinded by their loyalty to you. Cain and Raven would never stand up to you and say these things because you're their leader. You're in charge."

"So you're going to be that person to stand up to me, huh?"

North is looming over me a little, trying to intimidate me. I have to admit, it's kind of hot. But that doesn't mean I'm just going to roll over and let him win this argument.

I poke him in the chest, telling myself not to get distracted by his huge damn muscles.

"*Yes*, you dummy. I'm going to stand up to you. I'm calling you out on your stupid, self-destructive beliefs. You think beating yourself up is going to get you anywhere? Think again."

A stormy look passes over his face, his jaw muscles clenching. "You don't get to waltz in here and decide what I should and shouldn't do."

Our voices aren't rising, but they are getting sharper. We're almost right in each other's faces, our gazes locked and our teeth bared. I might not be a shifter, but I can snarl with the best of them.

"Why the fuck not?" I shoot back. "You made a huge deal about how we're mates. So why am I not allowed to care about you? To worry about you when I see you spiraling into a shitty thought pattern? Why don't I get to be a fucking part of your life?"

North jerks his head back as if startled. His eyes widen, and he growls at me, an expression I've never seen before passing over his face.

Then, faster than I can breathe, he grabs me, yanking me against him and kissing me.

CHAPTER 18

North's lips are hard and demanding on mine, and my body tenses in surprise at the suddenness of his kiss. My hands reach up to grip his shoulders automatically, holding on to keep my balance as my knees wobble a little.

He growls again, licking at the seam of my lips until I open for him, then plunging his tongue inside the moment I do. One large hand palms the back of my head, and he looms over me, angling his own head to take our kiss deeper.

I think I've forgotten how to breathe, but my body doesn't seem to mind the lack of oxygen. Why would it, when it can have *this*?

I haven't kissed North since that amazing night we all spent together, when he and his brothers owned my body in ways I had never imagined possible. I haven't kissed him since back when I still thought this thing between us was nothing but blazing sexual attraction, before I knew anything about the bond.

And fuck, I've missed it. I've missed the feeling of his lips, the taste of his skin, the way he makes me feel completely *dominated* in a way that somehow turns me on instead of scaring me.

I have no problem going toe-to-toe with him when it comes to an argument, but for some reason, I don't mind letting him take total control when it comes to this.

And he does.

He really fucking does.

Still kissing me like his life depends on it, North lets his hands roam over my body, his strong fingers squeezing and groping every bit of me. When he reaches down between us and slides his hand between my legs, cupping me there and grinding the heel of his hand against my clit, I whimper.

"Mine," he growls, pressing harder against my clit as his fingers slide along my pussy, teasing it through the fabric of my pants.

Fuck.

I'm still not sure how to feel about this bond that took me by complete surprise, but hearing him say that word in his deep, gravelly voice sends shockwaves through me. A rush of wetness dampens my panties as my heart starts to race wildly. There are too many emotions crashing around in my chest for me to sort through all of them, and in this moment, I don't even want to try.

I just want more of North.

More of this.

So I kiss him harder, shoving against the broad muscles of his chest as I press him back against the wall. He grunts, nipping at my bottom lip before plunging his tongue into my mouth. One large hand is still pressed between my legs, and I reach down to return the favor— but I do him one better, shoving my hand beneath the waistband of his pants and boxers so that my fingertips brush the smooth, hot skin of his cock.

North growls against my lips, sounding more wolf like than ever in this moment. His hips thrust against my touch even as he fists my hair with his free hand.

"Don't tease me, Kiara," he rumbles warningly.

"What makes you think I'm teasing?" I pant back, working my hand deeper into his pants until I can wrap my fingers around his thick length.

We're standing on the balcony of a hotel in Vegas, with his two brothers inside the hotel room only feet away. Not to mention the fact that although we're pretty high up, there are other hotels nearby that are almost as tall as this one. I didn't see anyone else on the balconies of the closest hotels, but that doesn't mean someone couldn't look out their window and see us.

But for some reason, I don't care.

Let them look if they want to.

To prove to North that I meant what I said, I stroke him again, rolling my hips against the hand trapped between my legs to get more friction on my clit at the same time.

"Fuck." He bites the word out before attacking my lips in another kiss, pulling me closer so that my chest is smashed up against his. "I want you so fucking much."

"Me too," I breathe, losing myself in how good it feels to finally give in. I've been craving him ever since that first time, and now it's like a dam has broken, sweeping us both away in a rushing torrent of pure, raw desire.

North wrenches his lips from mine, releasing his grip on my hair as he grabs my shoulders with both hands. He holds me at arm's length for a second, fire burning in his eyes. We're both breathing hard, and all the heightened emotion of our argument still crackles between us, filling the space with so many unspoken words that it's like being surrounded by a cacophony of whispered shouts.

I stare right back at him, holding his fierce gaze

without looking away. It feels like he's looking directly into my soul, making me feel vulnerable and laid bare, but that only cranks my desire up higher. I might as well be naked already for how exposed I feel under North's intense focus.

"I want you," I whisper, echoing his words. "I need you."

With another animalistic noise, North finally snaps into motion. Using his grip on my shoulders, he spins me around to face the railing. His large hands move frantically as he reaches down to fumble with the button and fly of my pants.

"Hands on the railing," he murmurs darkly, and I scramble to obey him, grabbing on to the metal rail to keep from falling as my entire body shakes with anticipation.

He doesn't even bother getting my pants all the way off. He just tugs them down over my hips and leaves them bunched up around my thighs before dragging my panties down too. Cool air hits my soaked pussy, and I hiss out a breath at the shock of sensation.

There's another rustling sound as North deals with his own clothes, and then his warm hands are back on my hips, his fingers digging into my flesh as he steps up behind me.

His broad cock slides between my legs, teasing my

folds and brushing against my clit, and we both groan.

"You feel so fucking good," he murmurs. "Better than I remember."

"You're not even inside me yet," I point out, shifting my hips to try to get the angle right so that my body will draw him in.

"So greedy." There's a pleased sort of taunt in his voice, and instead of thrusting into me, he keeps teasing me, sliding his cock back and forth between my pussy lips. "What do you want, Kiara? Tell me."

"Fuck—I want you—I—"

I move my hips again, baring my teeth in frustration as he refuses to breach my entrance.

"Use your words," North growls. "I know you can. You had a handful of them for me earlier, so I know you've got a mouth on you."

"You son of a bitch."

He hits my clit with his cock again, making my back arch. "Not the words I was looking for, baby girl."

God, this man truly is infuriating.

"Fuck me, North," I blurt, bumping my hips back against him. "Please."

"Good girl." He draws his hips back, and when he slides forward again, I can feel the thick head of his cock finally find my entrance. But then he pauses, barely inside me at all. "Fuck. Condom."

"It doesn't matter," I say quickly, practically sobbing by this point. "I'm on the pill. And I don't want anything between us. Please, I want to feel you."

As my words die out, North goes absolutely still for a heartbeat. I can't see his face, but I can *feel* the emotions rippling through his body anyway. Then he snaps his hips forward, driving into me in a single thrust.

I'm wet as hell from how worked up he's gotten me, but he's just as big as I remembered—bigger, even. There's an overwhelming stretch as he bottoms out inside me, and I almost lose my grip on the railing as my head drops forward.

"Shit," I pant. "Oh, holy shit. Holy fucking shit."

"You good?"

North's voice is like sandpaper, and I realize how much of the bond between us is on display right now. That bond is what's making him stop to check on me instead of just fucking me into oblivion like I'm pretty sure he wants to do.

But that's exactly what I want too.

"Yes," I gasp, forcing my head up enough to nod eagerly. "Yes. Just fuck me, North. Hard. Fast. Please."

Note to self: hard, fast, and please are magic words. At least as far as North is concerned.

Still holding my hips to keep me steady, the massive shifter draws out and then slams back into me so hard that both of us rock forward. He doesn't pause before doing it again, and again, and again, setting up a pace so hard and fast that I swear I can feel my teeth rattling.

And I fucking love it.

I've never exactly been a delicate flower, and after craving this man for so long without letting myself have what I wanted, it feels amazing to be completely consumed by him like this.

It feels different than the last time too, with nothing at all between us. I've never really minded condoms, but the feel of being skin to skin with him, of feeling the glide of his velvety cock against my inner walls, makes a torrent of heat pour through my veins.

"Do you feel that?" North drapes his upper body over mine, groping my breast with one large hand while the other loops around my waist. "It's like your body was fucking made for me. For us. You're so goddamn tight around my cock, Kiara. It's killing me."

I squeeze even harder around him, and he grunts, the steady rhythm of his thrusts hitching. The hand at my waist moves lower until his fingertips find my clit, and he pinches it lightly like he's showing me that two can play this game.

My toes curl in my shoes, and I bite my bottom lip so hard I'm afraid I'll break the skin. "Shit. North. Come on. Harder."

Apparently, I've been reduced to mostly one-word sentences. I don't really have the breath to get anything more out, and I'm a little surprised that North managed to say as much as he did a moment ago. He's breathing hard in my ear, his body straining behind mine, and I can feel my own muscles shaking from the exertion of trying to stay upright while he fucks me with everything he has.

"I'll give it to you harder," he promises. "I'll give you every fucking thing you want. But first, you have to come for me. I want to feel you come on my cock."

His fingers start working faster as he speaks, circling my clit with firm strokes. I'm practically clawing at the railing, my whole body bouncing as North pounds into me.

I *know* the other two men can hear us from inside the hotel room—not just the sounds of my whimpers and North's grunts, but the obscene sound of our bodies slapping together. But for some reason, when I think about them listening, when I imagine their reaction to hearing the man who's like their brother fucking me on the balcony, it just pushes me closer to the orgasm North just demanded of me.

"That's it," he encourages, as if he can feel how close I am. "Let go. Let go for me."

He slams into me one more time and stays there,

flicking his fingertip back and forth over my clit like I'm an instrument he knows exactly how to play. My inner walls clamp down around him as my back arches, an orgasm tearing through me like wildfire.

"North!" I half whisper, half scream his name, and he draws out and thrusts into me again.

"Don't hold back," he grunts. "I said let go."

"Fuck! *North!*"

This time, there's nothing whispered at all about my scream. It's a full-throated cry that comes from the very depths of me, echoing out over the Las Vegas landscape.

"Good girl," he growls, his voice rough and deep. "Now do it for me again."

With those words, he grabs my hips with both hands and picks up the pace again, giving me exactly what I was begging for earlier. He's no longer working my clit, but it doesn't matter. I'm so worked up, so overwhelmed by the feel of him behind me, inside me, his scent surrounding me, that I'm already close to coming again.

I'm breathing hard, clinging to the balcony as he drives into me, and when I feel his cock thicken, seeming to grow even harder than before, I let out a whimper.

"I'm coming. Oh god, I'm coming again," I moan as a new wave of pleasure pours through me.

"Yes. Fucking *yes.*"

North chokes out the words as he erupts inside me,

his cock pulsing and throbbing against my inner walls. I can feel the hot rush of his cum, and I'm so fucking glad he didn't use a condom.

I like this—way more than I should, probably, if I'm trying to keep my sanity around these men.

I like feeling marked by him.

Claimed by him.

I work my ass back against him, trying to bring him impossibly deeper as he empties himself inside me with a few more shuddering jerks. His front is draped over my back, and I can feel heat radiating from him like he's a furnace. I'm hot too, my skin covered with a light sheen of sweat from the unexpected workout. My heart is still racing, and I can feel the steady thud against my back that lets me know North's is too.

For several long beats, I don't move. I'm not entirely sure I *can* move yet, but more than that, I don't want this moment to end. I feel connected to North in a way I never have before, even when we had sex the first time.

That night with all three of them was hands down the hottest night of my life, but this is different than that. Because it's not just about sex, not just about pleasure.

It's about something a whole lot deeper.

Something I'm still a little scared of, but that part of me wants more than anything.

CHAPTER 19

Noth slowly pulls out of me, groaning as he does. He sounds like he hates to do it, like he'd stay buried inside me all day if it was an option, and I can't really blame him for that, because I get it.

Some of his cum drips down my inner thigh, and he reaches down to swipe it up with two fingers. But instead of cleaning his fingers off or something, he slides them back inside me, like he wants me to keep everything he gave me, even though I'm on the pill.

I clench around his fingers, a shiver working its way up my spine as my clit throbs all over again.

God, that's so dirty and possessive. Like a fucking caveman. Like a wolf trying to mark his territory.

So why do I like it so much?

North chuckles, pressing his fingers deeper before

pulling them out. He turns me around to face him, and when he holds up the two fingers he just had inside me, my stomach flutters. He's offering them to me.

I lick my lips, and the sexiest grin I've ever seen spreads across his face. He drags his fingers over my lips before slipping them in my mouth, and I swirl my tongue over them, cleaning off the rest of the cum.

Heat flares in his eyes as he watches me, and he makes sure I've gotten every bit of it before he withdraws his fingers. He helps me pull my pants back up before fixing his own, and when we're fully dressed again, he slides his fingers through my hair, tilting my face up as he drops his head to kiss me.

"I love that you can keep up with me," he murmurs when we break apart.

I laugh softly. "Honestly, I never really knew I was into exhibitionism until today."

He grins, although his eyes are serious. "Actually, neither did I. And to be honest, I kind of want to go door to door and kill any asshole who got a look at you or even *heard* you while we were fucking. But that's not what I mean."

My brows draw together. "What do you mean, then?"

"I mean what happened before the sex. I like that you push as hard as I do." He rolls his eyes, pulling a face. "I might not enjoy being called out on my bullshit, but... you're right. I need it. I need *you*."

His words hit me right in the chest, and I swallow.

Things are changing between me and North. Between me and all of these men, so fast.

Is this the bond? The mating connection? Is that what I'm feeling?

It should scare me, and it does a little, but not as much as before. I care about these men. They've all got something going on with them—Raven with his silence and his over-eagerness to please, Cain with his lack of trust, North with his self-esteem. I want to help them. They're good people and they're taking care of me.

I've only known these men for a few days, but it feels like I've known them for much longer. Like I should be worrying and caring about them. Like I'm going to know them so much longer. Like this is something real.

But can this be real? What about the vision I had when I first unlocked my Sight?

Dragging my lip through my teeth, I look up at North. "Are visions always true?"

"Fae visions?" he asks, sounding a bit surprised at my sudden change of topic.

I nod.

He sighs and tilts his head to look up at the sky. "I've never had it. The Sight. Even before my powers started…" He trails off, his jaw clenching. Then he shakes his head as if to clear it. "Anyway, I've never had it. So I don't know firsthand. But I've only ever heard of visions being true. I've never heard of one that was a lie, or completely inaccurate." He pauses. "You should ask Cain about this."

"But I'm asking you."

North gives me an amused quirk of his eyebrows, as if to say that he knows what I'm trying to do and he sees right through me, but he'll indulge me, just this once. "Well, Sight isn't super specific. It can be showing you something that you think is one thing, only it turns out to be another. It's not an exact science."

"So it's not that a vision is wrong, it's that someone could misinterpret it?"

He nods. "Yeah, pretty much."

"Sounds like a bit of a cop-out to me," I point out. "Oh, it's not the crazy magic we don't fully understand! We just didn't interpret it right!"

He snorts in amusement. "I see why you think that. But it's more like a math equation. When you don't understand how the math works, you come up with the wrong solution. But when you do know how it works, you can come up with the right solution. A vision is usually a math equation we don't know how to solve."

"I suppose." I'm still not sure. But I can't tell if my

reluctance is because of my skeptical nature or because of the way my heart hurts when I think about the vision I had.

If that vision really is of the future, then it's of a future where I'm all alone. And that shouldn't bother me, right? I'm used to being alone. But even though I'm still not sure in a lot of ways if I can accept this whole 'fated mate' business, having these three men here supporting me and caring for me means a lot more than I would've thought just a week ago.

"Everything all right?" North asks, his brows drawing together. "You smell... sad."

"You can *smell* my sadness? And here you were saying you had no powers," I tease.

"Having a slightly heightened sense of smell doesn't make me a true shifter," North growls, his ornery demeanor reasserting itself a bit.

I huff out a breath, arching a brow at him. "Still, that takes skill. To guess how someone's feeling. What does sadness smell like?"

North thinks for a moment. "Like when you're standing by a river and you can smell the water in the air. Like when you're eating something with mint and the mint is too strong, it hurts your teeth."

"Huh." I purse my lips, considering his answer for a moment. It's fascinating.

"It's just because people give off different pheromones depending on how they're feeling. Adrenaline, things like that." North looks uncomfortable, like he's worried I'll praise him again. Or maybe he's just unused to letting someone new in.

All three men seem to be struggling with that.

It's ironic. And frustrating. How can they be professing to keep me safe and look after me and be my fated mates when they won't open up to me?

At least they're not forcing me to open up to them, either. That's fair, I suppose.

North seems to have forgotten that I smelled sad, thank fuck. I don't know how to explain it to him. It's ridiculous, stupid even, to get attached to people so quickly. Right?

That's what I've always told myself.

"So I could see only part of what's actually happening," I say. "In my vision, I mean. I would have seen just part of something. Or I saw one thing and thought it meant another."

North nods. "Yeah. That's why some fae will pay someone to interpret their visions. They'll explain the vision and the person will do their best to explain it. Or they'll try to see what the fae saw. Visions are hard to interpret."

Relief sinks into me, like cool water flowing through my veins.

Okay then. My vision was just wrong.

Or rather, my interpretation of it was wrong. I don't *have* to be without the men. I just didn't see things right. That's all.

Before I can say anything else, the door to the balcony opens and Cain and Raven step out.

My stomach drops a little. Even though I know they're fine with sharing me, a part of me keeps waiting for signs of jealousy to appear.

It couldn't be more clear that North and I just had sex. Our clothes are disheveled, I screamed like a banshee when I came, and you don't need a shifter's senses to be able to smell the sex that lingers in the air.

But neither of the other two men look at all upset at what obviously just happened.

Rather than seeming angry, Cain and Raven's eyes are heated as they look at us, and I shiver. I'm tempted to go up to them and chase that heat. To feel it on my tongue. If this time with North made me feel as sated as the foursome did a couple days ago, I can't even imagine how sated and good I'll feel after having Cain and Raven as well.

I can see in their eyes that it would be easy. All I'd have to do would be to kiss them, slide my hands down between their legs and start to massage them through their pants. They're already half hard, from the look of things.

But despite the urges of my body and the hungry looks on their faces, now isn't the time. Cooler heads have to prevail.

Fucking North was a great tension reliever, and it sure seemed to help him get out of his head. God knows he needed that. But we still have to make a plan. There's still a vampire mob boss after me, and still a missing Aurora Gem.

As if coming to the same conclusion, Cain tears his gaze away from us, blinks for a second, and seems to get himself back under control.

"Raven and I have been coming up with a plan," he says, looking back at us.

I perk up immediately, my heart jumping in my chest. "Really?"

I honestly didn't expect that. Not that I doubt them, but I sure don't have a plan.

"Good," North says. He gestures toward the door. "We should go inside to discuss it."

As I enter back into the suite, the men all form around me, like I'm the sun and they're planets in orbit. It's almost like I can feel them even without touching them. Is this the fated mate bond that they were talking about? Is this the connection?

"You guys know that you don't have to stick around," I remind them, guilt twisting in my stomach. "You don't have to chain yourselves to a sinking ship."

All three men look at me like I'm being completely ridiculous. "You're not a sinking ship," Cain says. "And of course we're going to help you."

"Did you find another Aurora Gem?" I point out. "Because unless you did—"

"We're not giving up," Raven says emphatically. He then looks over at North, like he's feeling he spoke out of turn.

North nods at him supportively, then looks at me. "We're not giving up and leaving you. Not until you're safe. If you don't want us around after that..."

He trails off and pauses, glancing at the other two men. It's clear that none of them like the idea of leaving me at all. My heart twists. I've never had anyone be so loyal to me, to want to stay around me. Look, I know I'm not exactly the friendliest of people. I don't always get along well with everyone. I keep to myself.

But these guys are looking out for me anyway. Even if I'm not sugar and spice and everything nice.

"If you don't want us around after that," North

repeats, "then we'll leave you alone. If that's what you really want. But we're making sure you're safe first."

I'm not used to this. Not at all.

Still, as I look at these three men and their earnest faces, I can't help but think that maybe, just maybe, I *could* get used to it.

CHAPTER 20

Before we get down to business, I duck into the bathroom quickly to clean up, then emerge a few moments later to rejoin the men. Raven and Cain are settled on one couch in the large suite, so I sit next to North on the one facing it.

"Okay." I lean forward eagerly, trying to temper the hope that beats against my chest. "What's your plan?"

"We used our Sight to try to find another Aurora Gem," Cain says. "But we couldn't find one."

Now that I look at them more closely, I can see that they look a lot more tired than they did before I went out onto the balcony. There are shadows under their eyes. North and I weren't exactly having a sex marathon out there, but we weren't just having a quickie, either. And we had a whole conversation before and after. Did Cain and Raven use their Sight that entire time?

They must be exhausted. And they did that for *me*. My heart thumps loudly, and I swallow around the sudden tightness in my throat. Even if they weren't able to find another gem, it means a lot to me that they tried.

"It's okay," I tell them. "I'll figure something else out. Honestly. You don't have to try to find a gem for me."

"No, we don't," Cain agrees. "But you don't have to figure something else out, either."

"What?" What does he mean? Of course I have to. Donovan's not just going to give up on me.

"You don't have to give him an Aurora Gem," Cain explains, "because we have something even better to give him."

I scramble to think what that could be. What could possibly be better than an Aurora Gem? What could make up for Donovan's loss?

Cain smirks triumphantly and looks at North.

North raises his eyebrows, and I can tell that he's thinking hard. Then he nods at Cain, as if giving permission.

I've never been jealous of their bond before, but right now I sure would like to know what they're all thinking, since they seem to be on the same page and don't need words.

"Anything you guys want to share with the class?" I ask, looking back and forth between all of them. "Clearly you've agreed on something. Mind letting me know what it is?"

Cain looks at me. "We can give him an Immortal Key."

That brings me up short. "You've got to be kidding me. Where the hell would we get an Immortal Key? Those are even more rare than Aurora Gems, are you guys out of your minds?"

I look around at the three of them, but all of the men seem deadly serious. Okay, so maybe they know something that I don't. Maybe they've got a friend who has an Immortal Key and just for some reason will be willing to give it to them—or more likely, they know how to steal it from them.

But as far as I know, those things are even more rare than Aurora Gems. You have to be pretty damn powerful to have one. They're the sort of thing that are just rumored about. I've sure never laid hands or eyes on one, and I don't know anyone who has.

The men all look at me with this sly gleam in their eyes.

"We don't need to go looking for an Immortal Key," Cain informs me. "We already have one."

I stare at him in shock. "You've got to be kidding me."

"I wish we were," Raven grumbles. "Thing's more trouble than it's worth."

"Now, now," Cain says, patting Raven on the knee. "It was sort of our nest egg. Our emergency fund, I suppose you could say. Something to keep for a rainy day."

"You wouldn't want to, I don't know, keep an umbrella instead?" I ask, half-joking.

North shakes his head. "We're serious, Kiara. We have an Immortal Key."

"How could you possibly?" I blurt out. "Not that—I don't mean any offense, guys, you're clearly not just bumming it off the streets, but Immortal Keys—vampire kings have them, those kinds of people! How did you get a hold of one?"

"We were doing a bounty hunting job years back," Cain says. "And we... didn't really like who was currently the owner of it. So we took it."

"Nobody knew it was us," North adds.

"And we've been keeping it hidden and safe ever since," Cain finishes. "Nobody expected us to have something like that. Like you said, only really powerful people tend to be able to get their hands on an Immortal Key and keep it from being taken from them. We've kept it under lock and... well, key." He smirks at his own joke. "For years now."

"And nobody knows about it?"

He shakes his head. "Nope. Nobody."

That's impressive. I mean, most people don't know who has Immortal Keys, they're so rare. But if you do have one you need to be careful about it and hide it well because if other people have even a whiff you've got one they'll come to steal it from you. That's why only extremely powerful people are said to have them.

Then the rest of what they're saying catches up to me. "Wait. Are you saying you'd give Donovan O'Shae your Immortal Key?"

"Yes," North confirms. "It's more important than an Aurora Gem. He can consider your debt cleared."

A lump forms in my throat, and I swallow hard. "You can't be serious."

"Do I look like the kind of person who jokes about these kinds of things?" North replies.

"But if you give that up—it's your ticket out of— anything. Your get out of jail free card. Your emergency fund." I shake my head. "You've already risked your lives to help me, I can't let you do this too."

"There's no 'letting' us about it," North says firmly. "We're going to give it to you. If it will save you..."

"You're supposed to use it to save *your* asses," I point out. "Not mine."

"It's ours," Cain says. "That means we get to use it how we choose to, and this is how we're choosing to use it. You can't stop us from doing that."

I open my mouth to argue—but then pause. He does have a point. "Well, I can refuse your help."

"You could," Cain acknowledges.

Damn it. It's like they know I'll say yes. And I suppose I have to. What other choice do I have? Try to find an Aurora Gem or another equally valuable replacement while fighting off bounty hunters? That's no life. I'll lose eventually and the cost will be my existence.

I sigh, and the men get triumphant looks on their faces—they know they've won. Damn it. "Fine. I don't think I'm worth it, but it's your choice, it's your key."

"Sorry, what was that you were saying to me earlier?" North asks. "About knowing your worth? Not downplaying it?"

I flip him off, but I'm struggling to hide down a smile. "How dare you throw my own words back at me?"

North takes my hands, not letting me slide into joke territory. "You are worth ten times more than an Immortal Key, or any other artifact. A hundred times more."

My heart is thumping in my chest so loudly that I'm sure all three of the men can hear it, hell, the people who have the suite next door to us can probably hear it. I feel like I might cry. And I don't cry in front of people. I just don't.

"Really, are you sure? You—you have to be sure. Something like this you can't take back."

"Kiara," Raven says, final speaking up, "when are you going to realize that we'd do anything for you?"

My heart feels like it's breaking. He's so goddamn earnest. Is it just this 'fated mate' thing that's making me feel this way?

But what if fated mates are just bullshit? I've never heard of them. I was telling the truth earlier when I said that. What if I'm right, and fated mates are just something that the men believe in, but they aren't actually real?

That means that whatever I'm feeling right now— my heart shifting in my chest, like someone's wrapped a string around it and tugged—it could be up to anything. I don't know if it's fate or not. But I'm being taken care of by these men. They're risking their lives for me and helping me out even though they barely know me.

I can't help but think that, whatever the reason, it almost doesn't matter. I feel how I feel. I don't know how to say it out loud. But the emotions welling up inside me, pushing up against me from the inside? I can feel those. And they feel real. I can't deny that.

I wish I had the words to express this sensation, but I'm not used to this. It's sad, honestly. I've been alone so long I don't know how to tell people that I care about them? That I appreciate them?

But there is another way, without words, that I can make my emotions known.

I turn to North and put my hands on his face, framing it, and draw him into me. Surprise flashes over his face, but then I kiss him, and he melts. Like it's already a habit for him to kiss me, like he already knows that this is how it's supposed to be.

I wish I had that kind of faith, but I think maybe I'm starting to learn how to.

North gets his hands on my hips and pulls me into his lap as we kiss, the kiss turning heated until I pull away with a gasp. Cain and Raven are watching, heat back in their gazes, and I get up from the couch and go over to them.

Raven doesn't move. He stares up at me like I'm made of starlight, his eyes dark and wide, and I sit on his lap and take his face in my hands just as I did with North. Raven knows what's coming, and he wraps his arm around my waist to anchor me as I kiss him, sweet and deep.

I turn away, toward Cain, who's already standing up. He yanks me to him, and I kiss him with passion and fervor, hanging onto the front of his shirt. I can feel Raven and North watching, seeing Cain's hands as they slide down to grab my ass, and I shiver.

By the time I break away, I'm breathing hard, and so is Cain.

I can feel the heat of the gazes from the other two like a physical touch, like fingers trailing down my spine.

"Do we... have to leave to get the key right now?" I ask, my voice a little husky. "Or can it wait a little while?"

I don't have a concealment charm, so I'm wary of more bounty hunters finding us. But I'm pretty sure the temple or whatever it's called that we were just at is untraceable, so we were untraceable while we were there. That probably bought us some extra time.

And if we have any extra time at all, I damn sure know how I want to spend it.

Cain smiles, flashing me the reckless, devilish grin that I'm starting to love so much. "I think we can probably spare a few minutes. Why? What did you have in mind?"

My stomach clenches, desire shooting through me like a firework bursting in the sky.

"You three have helped me so much, and now you're

going to do even more. I want to thank you properly. *All* of you."

CHAPTER 21

The heat of North and Raven's gazes seems to increase tenfold, scorching my skin and making goosebumps rise up all over me.

Cain's teasing smile slips away a little as fierce desire rises up in his expression, and he pulls me closer before dropping his head to skim his nose along the side of my neck.

"Fuck, Kiara," he groans. "Even if bounty hunters were standing outside the door ready to try to take us out right this second, I don't think I could say no to you. Do you have any idea how badly we all want you? How much we've craved you since that night?"

I do have some idea, actually, since I've been craving them too—whether I was ready to admit it to myself or not.

"So is that a yes?" I ask, my eyes rolling back a little as he darts his tongue out to taste my skin.

"It's a fuck yes. A hell yes. A 'let the rest of the world burn, I won't even care as long as I have this' yes."

I laugh, then gasp as he replaces his tongue with his teeth, biting gently at the spot where my neck meets my shoulder.

Raven and North close in on either side of us, surrounding me in hard male bodies. I have a moment to wonder how on earth this became my life before three sets of hands start roaming over me, three pairs of lips caressing my skin. Then it becomes hard to think about anything, to focus on anything but the feel of them.

Just like with North on the balcony outside, this feels *different*. Because all of us know by now that this isn't just a one-night stand. We've been through some crazy shit together, and we know each other so much better than we did that night.

I care about these men, and I want to make them feel as good as they make me feel.

I want them to know how grateful I am.

With only two hands compared to their six, I'm not able to grope them as thoroughly as they touch me. I want to touch all of them at once, but I settle for moving from one man to the next and back again, kissing whoever I can reach before breaking apart to seek out a new set of lips.

I get lost in it for a while, pleasure building steadily in my veins like a pot coming to a boil, giving myself over to how good it feels to be surrounded and worshipped.

The sex I had with North on the balcony seems like it happened a long time ago now—or at least, my body keeps trying to convince me it did. I should feel worn out and sated by our intense fuck, but I don't. I feel hungry, and judging from the hardness that presses against my belly as North pulls me close for another kiss, he's just as hungry as I am.

They move me between them, passing me off to each other willingly as they turn me around in the small circle created by their bodies. When I'm handed off to Raven, he slides his hands down over my waist and hips and then grips my ass, lifting me up. My legs wrap around him instinctively, and the other two men step back, giving him room to move.

I expect him to carry me toward the bed, but instead, he brings me over to the couch. He sets me down on the arm at one end, and I watch with my breath caught in my throat as he kneels in front of me.

Cain crawls up onto the couch behind me, tugging my shirt off while Raven works on my pants and panties. I shift my weight a little to help them both, and when

I'm just in my bra, Cain reaches around to palm my breasts as Raven slides his hands up my bare thighs.

"I can smell you," Cain whispers in my ear, rolling my nipples between his fingers. "I can smell the sex on you, even though you tried to clean it up. I can smell the fresh arousal on you too. Is Raven going to find you wet for us, Kiara?"

"Yes," I breathe. I can tell it's true. I can feel the slickness gathering in my core, and I feel almost desperate for Raven to put his mouth on me and lap it up.

"Good. Because we're all hard as hell for you," Cain murmurs, undoing my bra and tossing it aside. "Look at North. He was just inside you, and already, he's dying for more."

I glance upward as Raven runs his tongue up my inner thigh, shivering as I catch sight of North standing off to one side, cupping the bulge of his hard cock as he stares at us. I lick my lips, reaching out for him to draw him closer, but he shakes his head.

A small smile curves his lips, his dark blue eyes flashing. "Uh uh, baby girl. I'm good right where I am. I want to watch my brothers make you fall apart. I want to see everything they do to you."

As if inspired by North's words, Raven chooses this

moment to finally bury his face between my legs, dragging his tongue up and down over my clit.

"Shit!" I yelp, my upper body falling backward a little as the shock of sensation courses through me. Cain is right there to catch me though, holding me up as Raven presses my thighs wider apart and devours me like he's starving.

Cain's lips find the side of my neck, and I know he's watching what Raven is doing to me just like North is.

North said he wanted to watch them make me fall apart, and it feels like that's exactly what's about to happen. My legs are quivering already, my heart racing, and I can't stop myself from reaching down to grip the silky strands of Raven's black hair.

"Come on my face," he growls, clamping his lips around my clit and lashing the tip of his tongue back and forth.

I arch my back, leaning against Cain for support as an orgasm rips through me. My nerve-endings are still extra sensitive from when North fucked me on the balcony, so it feels like pure heat is pouring through my veins as I writhe between Raven and Cain.

When it finally begins to subside, Raven looks up at me through his thick lashes, still toying with my clit with the tip of his tongue. His lips and chin are a bit wet, glistening in the overhead light, and I shiver at the sight of him like this.

"Take off your clothes," I whisper hoarsely. "All of you."

Considering how stubborn and bossy these men can be—particularly North—I'm not sure they'll obey me. But as Cain helps me find my balance on the couch's arm again, Raven stands up and begins stripping off his clothes. North joins him, and once he's sure I'm steady, Cain rises from the couch and practically tears his clothes off, clearly not wanting to be the last one naked.

As North shucks his pants and kicks them away, I stare raptly at the sight before me. It's just as stunning as the last time I saw them all like this.

Seriously, if you ever have a chance to find yourself surrounded by three gorgeous, muscled, completely naked men?

Take. It.

Since the guys already got my clothes off, we're all even now. I stand up slowly and walk toward them, and the three of them close in around me as if they've been drawn toward me by a magnetic force.

Trapping my lower lip between my teeth, I shoot them a teasing, mischievous look. Then I drop down to my knees in the center of the rough circle they've made with their bodies.

Three massive, hard cocks are now directly at my eye level, and my pussy clenches as I glance around.

"Well, well, well." I tilt my head up to look at the men. "Isn't this a gorgeous sight?"

Cain chuckles, and North makes a sound like a growl. Raven reaches down to squeeze his cock, which is already leaking droplets of precum, but I reach out and tug his hand away, shaking my head.

"Let me do it," I murmur.

He hisses out a breath as I replace his hand with my own, wrapping my fingers around him as much as I can and sliding my fist up and down his length. The precum helps slick the way, but I need more lube, so I wrap my lips around him and bob my head as I work my fist over his length in tandem with my mouth.

He grunts, his hips thrusting forward so that his cock hits the back of my throat. I gag a little but don't stop, squeezing him harder. I can feel the veins pulsing along his length, feel him getting harder in my mouth, but I don't suck him hard enough to make him come just yet.

Instead, I pull back after a moment and turn toward Cain.

He grins down at me, holding his hands up as if to prove that he's perfectly willing to let me be the only one to touch his cock right now.

"Will you kiss it?" he asks teasingly. "Make it feel better?"

I grin, leaning in to press a chaste kiss to the tip of his cock. He makes a satisfied sound as I slowly wrap my mouth around him, going down as far as I can as my lips spread around his thick girth.

"God, you look so good with your mouth full of my cock," he groans, and I hear the other two men let out quiet moans as well.

I can't answer with words, so I just give him a bit of a show, sliding my lips up and down his length as I hollow my cheeks. I don't let him get too close to coming before I pull away, turning to North last.

North, in typical North fashion, doesn't tease me or wait for me to tease him. He just palms the back of my head, bringing my mouth to his cock and helping me slide down as far as I can take.

"So fucking good," he groans, and the ragged sound of his voice makes my clit throb.

I relax my throat as much as possible, letting him guide my motions as I bob my head. Blindly, I reach out toward the other two men, wrapping a hand around each of them and stroking lightly, wanting to touch them all at once.

I switch off a few more times, rotating between them until their grunts start getting deeper, their cocks slicked with saliva and precum. They're getting close, I can tell, all three of them. And even though this was only meant to be part of the warm-up, I'm struck with the sudden urge to bring them all over the edge this way, to feel them come one after another, to let them mark me up as I kneel between them.

But before I can make that particular fantasy happen, Cain draws back a little and then reaches down, plucking me up as if I weigh nothing.

"Nice try, darling." He grins. "But when I finish, I want it to be inside you."

Pressing his lips to mine, he carries me to the bed this time, then sets me down gently on the mattress. All three men climb up with me, and when Cain lies down on his back, I don't waste my opportunity. I roll over and straddle his waist, resting my hands on his chest as I slide my wet pussy over his cock.

He hisses out a breath, gripping my hips. "Close. But not quite."

With a chuckle, I reach down and fist his length. I rise up higher on my knees, lining him up with my entrance.

"No condom," I whisper. "North didn't use one, and I don't want you to either. Is that okay?"

I swear he almost chokes, his fingers digging harder into my hips. "Holy fuck. Yes, that's more than okay. But you better put me inside you right now, because I'm about to come just from *thinking* about it."

God, these men are good for my ego.

With a sly smile, I slowly start to sink down onto him, taking him into my body inch by inch. His eyes roll back a little, the muscles in his neck standing out as his nostrils flare. Once he's fully seated, I rise up and sink back down a few times, giving us both the friction we need.

"You want to get my brothers in on this?" Cain murmurs, sliding his hands up to cup my breasts. "I can share you with Raven, and North can take your mouth. We all want you so much, Kiara."

"Yes. Please!"

I nod vigorously, feeling the heat at my back as Raven slips into place behind me. I splay my hands on the bed on either side of Cain's head as Raven grabs my hips and pulls me off his friend's cock. He slides into my core instead, filling me in a smooth stroke as I brace myself of all fours.

The feel of being momentarily empty and then being filled so completely again makes me whimper, and North chuckles as he comes to kneel beside us. His fingers tangle in my hair, and he uses that grip to turn my head toward him.

"Open for me, baby girl," he says, his voice a low purr.

I do, dropping my jaw and twisting my neck a little more to get the right angle to take him into my mouth. I can't really use a hand to assist without losing my balance, but he doesn't seem to mind that one bit as I swirl my tongue over his smooth crown.

Raven slides out of me, and Cain helps me sink back down onto his cock again. My clit grinds against him as he bottoms out inside me, and I make a soft noise around North's shaft.

The man beneath me and the one behind me trade off again, working in such perfect tandem that I can't believe they've never done this before. They keep switching back and forth, sliding into me one after the other, fucking me harder each time.

When Cain slides into me again, I yelp when I feel broad fingertips slide between my ass cheeks. North tightens his grip on my hair, and Raven chuckles. His finger presses against my back hole, sliding inside just a little way.

"Maybe one day Cain and I will take you at the same time," Raven murmurs. "Maybe you'll take one of us here and one of us in your pussy. Would you like that?"

Would I?

It's not really something I've ever considered before. My sex life with Jason was fairly vanilla, but these three men have unlocked a side of me I never knew existed. A side that feels almost insatiable, a side that always wants more.

And that side is screaming *"yes!"*

I nod as much as possible, pressing back against Raven's hand to bring his finger deeper into my ass. All three men react, and Raven gives me what I want, starting to fuck me gently with his finger as Cain keeps thrusting up into my core.

The blowjob I'm giving North has gotten messy as I've gotten more distracted and turned on, and I refocus on him, trying to channel everything I'm feeling into the way I slide my lips up and down his shaft.

"You should see your face right now, darling," Cain rasps, his breath coming faster. "I can tell you like what Raven is doing."

I do like it. It feels strange but really good, a more complete feeling of fullness than I've ever experienced before. Raven keeps moving his finger in and out of my ass, and I pick up the telltale sound of him sliding his free hand over his cock as he adds a second finger in my back hole. He grunts softly, and I flush at the thought of what kind of view he's getting right now.

"Shit, this is too good." Cain shakes his head, grimacing. "I'm gonna come soon. I can't hold back any longer. Make North come too, Kiara. Then Raven will let go."

The idea of them all finishing at once is a pure aphrodisiac, and I hollow my cheeks and bob my head as I work to bring North to climax. I can feel the tension rising between all four of us, all of us careening headlong toward our orgasms.

"Oh fuck. Fuck. Fuck!" North shouts.

His cock pulses against my tongue, flooding my mouth with a rush of cum, and a second later, Cain pulls me down hard on his cock, arching his back as he finishes too.

"Yes," Raven mutters from behind me. "Fuck yes."

He drags his fingers out of my ass, and I can hear the strokes of his other hand getting faster and more desperate as he jerks himself off to release. Warm, wet cum spatters against my skin, and I shudder at the feel of it, heat blooming in my core.

The heat expands outward as my orgasm hits me like a ton of bricks. My mouth slides off North's cock, and I let out a hoarse cry as I come hard, surrounded by all three men.

I collapse onto Cain's chest, and he rolls us over onto our sides as Raven settles behind us. North collapses to the mattress too, reaching out to stroke my hair.

"You don't owe us any thanks," he says, and I tilt my

head a little to look into his dark blue eyes. "We will protect you, always. It's our privilege and our duty as your mates." His full lips quirk up at the corners. "But you're always welcome to express your appreciation for us."

I laugh, feeling lighter than I have in a long time. Maybe it's silly, since we've still got bounty hunters after us, and we haven't even gotten the Immortal Key yet. But we have a plan.

We have a plan.

Not just me, but all four of us.

I drag my lower lip between my teeth, unable to contain my smile as Raven moves closer and nuzzles my neck.

"Deal," I say.

CHAPTER 22

As much as I'd love to spend several hours in bed napping, cuddling, or... doing other stuff, we don't have *that* much time, unfortunately.

We've pushed it about as far as we can, so after a few minutes, we all clamber out of bed and clean up quickly, then throw our clothes back on.

Once we're all gathered back in the main part of the suite, we begin to open up another portal, to our farthest destination yet. I'm not sure I could open a portal that goes this far on my own, but that could just be my inexperience with magic.

"At first, we wanted to put the Key in our apartment," Cain explains as we set up the portal. "That way it was close and we could keep a direct eye on it. But then we realized that having something like that in the city where others could possibly magically detect it was a bad idea."

"We didn't want assholes sniffing around," North growls. "So we decided to put the key far away from any settlements."

"Nobody could accidentally stumble on it," Cain says. "Nobody could even think to try to detect for it. It would be in the middle of nowhere."

"Makes it hard for us to get to it," North adds. "But we don't need to get to it quickly anyway. Or so we thought."

I feel a flash of guilt, but there's nothing accusatory or judging in North's tone. He's just stating facts.

The portal opens, and with it comes a blast of cold that's entirely at odds with the heat of Vegas. I shiver, and Raven puts his hand on my shoulder comfortingly.

North leads the way through the portal, then Cain. I go in next, and then Raven follows. I put my hand up, shielding my face, squinting through the bitterly cold air and the snow as I step through the portal and onto the slope of a mountain, one in a long chain.

"Welcome to the Himalayas," Cain says, shouting a little to be heard over the wind that whips around us, carrying flurries of snow with it.

I feel like the characters in *Lord of the Rings* when

they're on that mountain. I'm going to be covered in snow and turned into a popsicle before long.

The portal closes behind us with a snap, and I shiver as the cold really hits me. I am definitely not dressed for this kind of thing. None of the guys are, either. Cain must be especially miserable. Demons like heat, they get cold easily. No prizes for guessing why.

But if Cain is unhappy, he isn't complaining. "This way," he says, waving his hand to indicate for me to follow him.

I do follow him, shivering all the way, as North looks around as if he thinks that someone might've actually followed us onto this godforsaken middle-of-nowhere spot.

Wings wrap around me, shielding me from the wind and snow, and I look behind me to see that Raven's partially transformed. He's not fully stone, but he's looking less normal now, horns and claws and fangs out, his wings keeping me safe.

North and Cain lead the way, Raven shielding me. The snow is all the way up to my waist, and I have to step carefully. It's clear that no human has been on this mountain range in ages, possibly ever. I feel the way with my feet, but I'm not sure that I'm actually even touching the ground. My feet could just be on more hard-packed snow for all that I can tell. The thought is chilling. Just one wrong step, or even a harsh wind, and I'll go tumbling down the mountain into the air, into freefall.

Raven puts his hands on my shoulders. He might not talk much but he seems to know how I'm feeling. I shoot him a grateful look over my shoulder. I've been at the top of buildings before but this is nerve-wracking.

"Should be around here somewhere," Cain says. Right as he does, only a few steps ahead of him, North drops into the snow.

Literally. He takes a step, and then he's just gone.

My jaw falls open, and it's only my training as a thief that keeps me from screaming. If something scares or startles you on a job and you scream, you're a fucking goner. But what the fuck just happened?

Cain, to my shock, doesn't react except to take a few steps forward after North and then he's disappearing too. Just like that they've vanished as if they were never there.

"What the—North! Cain!" I yell. I can't hold my shock in anymore. My heart is pounding. Where are they? What just happened?

"It's all right," Raven says. He scoops me up into his arms, and then he's taking a few steps forward too, and to my embarrassment I scream as the world drops away and we fall.

Raven lands neatly on his feet, still holding me, and then sets me carefully on my feet. I look up and around, and I realize that we're in a hidden ice cave.

The cave itself has smooth walls all around us, a pale white-blue from the ice. There's just enough light from up above to see by, which is good because I don't think Cain could use his fireball to help us see, under these circumstances.

"Originally we chose Everest," Cain says. "An easy marker to get a portal to, easy to focus on and remember. But Everest has become absolutely choked with tourists. There are waiting lines to get to the summit and people die on there constantly. We figured the chances of someone stumbling on the Key, or a supernatural person on a vacation detecting it, was too great. So we chose this ice cave a couple of peaks over."

That makes sense. '

North makes his way directly to the back of the cave, crouching down onto his knees and brushing some of the snow on the floor out of the way. "We set up a lot of traps too. Just in case."

I stay back as North presses his hand down into the snow. I can't see exactly what happens, but I hear something that sounds like a click and then a moment later, the back of the ice cave slides open.

Raven and Cain walk up and join North at the

mouth of this entrance. Bit by bit, the three of them undo whatever magical protections they put in place. Some of the protections seem to only need one of them, but a specific one. I get the impression that certain locks can only be opened by Cain, for example, and that if Raven or North tried, it wouldn't work. There are also a few that only open when all three men open them at the same time using the same motions.

It would be impossible, or so it seems, for someone else to get in. You would need all three men to cooperate with you, and I don't see these men giving into someone else and letting that person steal from them no matter what.

"Can I watch?" I ask. I'm wildly curious. This would be a dream for me to try to break into. I could really challenge myself. I mean, having to break into this for a job would piss me off like nothing else, and I doubt I would actually accept the job, given the level of security, but just for fun? I would love it.

North gives me a look like he knows what I'm thinking. "When it wouldn't kill you to come close, then yes, you can try to break this open."

"That's not what I said."

"That's what you were thinking."

I grin. It's only been a few days but he clearly already knows me too well. He knows my tricks.

"Okay," North calls. "You can come up."

I walk over to them. I'm so cold I can't stop shivering, my teeth clacking together. I curl up into Raven, who curls a wing around me again. We really should've brought coats or something for this.

With the protections gone, now I can see into the hidden room and find that there's a huge block of ice taking up almost the entire space. Inside of the ice, right in the center of it, is a key.

Looking at it, you wouldn't think that it was an Immortal Key. An Immortal Key is basically a skeleton key for literally anything. Magical, mundane, whatever. As a burglar, if I had one of these, I could open anything. Supposedly all you have to do is hold the key up and think about what you want opened, and it opens. And I really do mean anything. I don't know for sure because I've never had one, but I hear you can open people's thoughts and mouths, get them to tell you truths.

But this just looks like an ordinary key. A bit tarnished. I can't tell what metal it's made out of. But it's not big or flashy, not made out of solid gold. Fascinating.

Cain walks up and lights a fireball in his hand, pressing it to the block of ice. Fueled by demonic heat, the ice quickly melts, much faster than it would if someone else were to try that. Cain presses his hand farther and farther in, until he's reached the key and can grab it and retract his hand.

The key looks perfectly normal in his palm. He holds it out to me to look at. "You want to test it out?" Cain teases.

I shake my head. I don't need to do that, thanks. And the idea of holding something so powerful in my hand kind of gives me the heebie-jeebies. I just give my magical items that I steal over to my fence. I don't actually use them myself.

Cain hands the key to North, who pockets it and nods. He reaches down into the snow again and closes up the hidden panel. "If we ever need to hide anything else here. We've still got this place set up," he points out.

That's good. But seeing this key, just feeling the power of it that radiates off of it, makes me uneasy. Is it really a smart idea to give this up to someone like O'Shae? It could put the men in a bad position, and it will take away their one safeguard. They could be using this for themselves, not for me.

"We need to get out of here before we portal out," North says. "Can't risk anyone finding this place by having residue of a portal here."

"Wait." I grab onto Raven so that he doesn't grab me and lift me up out of the cave. "You shouldn't do this, any of you. I can't let you do this. I have to take care of this. I'll find a way. I always do."

"Of course you can find a way," Raven says. He smiles warmly at me. Even with his face like that of a gargoyle, his smile makes his face light up, and I melt a little.

Raven takes my hands and squeezes them. "You're our mate. Of course you're resourceful. It's not about what you can and can't do. It's about what you don't have to do. And we're here now. Of course you can do this on your own, but you don't have to. That's the whole point of having us and having mates."

My heart swells. I really don't have anything to add to that. What could I possibly add? All of my emotions are cramming up in my throat, so I just swallow. "Thank you."

I kiss him, short and sweet, and then the other two. I don't let it get heated because this is definitely not the place for it. I don't care how hot the guys are, I'm not taking what few clothes I have off in this weather.

"Shall we head on home, then?" Cain says.

Home. What an idea. Could I really have a home with other people, with these men, after this?

"Okay," I agree. "Let's do this."

I take a shaky breath and let Raven carry me out of the ice cave.

CHAPTER 23

We take the portal back to New York City. We're exhausted from all of the traveling, and we could go back to the safe house to get some rest under the safety of the concealment charm, but I don't want to waste any time and neither do the men. We want this over with.

At least there's going to be no trouble in finding Donovan O'Shae's headquarters. A lot of criminals like to hide out where they can't be found. But once you get to a certain level of power, why hide? You know that nobody's going to come after you. And there's some merit to having a semblance of respectability. If you want to have a conversation in public, you don't go to an empty pub or a park. You go to a busy restaurant or some other place that has so many people around it you blend in.

Donovan's taken that route. His place is a large fancy law firm, or what looks like a large fancy law firm. Nobody ever actually stumbles inside. There are magical wards in place so that if you start to go in and you're human, not supernatural, you get this terrible feeling in your stomach like impending doom and you find an excuse to turn around and leave.

"I don't know what I was thinking," I murmur as we approach. "Thinking that I could break in here and get away with it."

"You didn't know how powerful he was," Cain replies. "It's all right. We all make mistakes."

"Yeah, but my mistake might cost us all our lives."

North shakes his head. "Not with this key, it won't," he assures me. "Although. I'm impressed you got through all of this security. I can smell the layers of magic on it."

"I didn't go through here," I reply. "I went in through the back. I was following a tracking spell to find the Aurora Gem for my client, and I got in through a back door. If I'd seen the front of this place, I probably would've had a better idea of what kind of person I was stealing from."

It was a rookie mistake, not doing my research. I should have known better.

"Donovan keeps his cards close to the chest," North says. "Things have been changing in the vampire world lately. It's not a surprise that you didn't know. We all fuck up sometimes. What matters is that we're here to help you fix it. You're cleaning up your mess. That's what's important."

I take a few deep breaths. I suppose North is right. It's inevitable that I'll fuck up. What's important is that I'm fixing it. Right. "I don't suppose we could tell that to Donovan and he'll be more lenient with me?" I joke.

North snarls, and so does Raven. "He'll be lenient with you," Raven says. "If he knows what's good for him."

I've never heard Raven sound like that. I put a hand on his arm. "Easy, big boy. I can't have you starting a whole blood war on my behalf, tempting as it is."

"We're going to be fine," North assures us.

We approach the steps of the building, and I can feel the ripple of magic passing through my body as we walk up the steps to the front door. Looking up, I can sense some of the various magical protections.

I try the front door. It's locked.

"We could try knocking," Cain suggests.

"We could try the back way. The one that I used to sneak in."

North shakes his head. "We'll look like we're here

to cause more trouble. This is just a deterrent. The real entrance will be somewhere to the side. Follow me."

We all fall into step, with Raven keeping an arm around me. We could be attacked at any moment and it feels like every hair on my body is standing on end. Donovan could see us and recognize me and just straight-up attack us. But I'm not sure that he knows what I look like. I wasn't seen when I stole the gem, it was just that he figured out my identity. He might think we're four random people.

Or, well, not so random. I get the feeling that these three men have been around long enough, Donovan will have an idea who they are.

North leads us down an alley, looking around, until he approaches a dumpster. I see it as he walks up: the dumpster is bolted to the ground.

Dumpsters have to be able to move or roll so that they can be pushed into the streets for the garbage truck on garbage day. This one's bolted which means it needs to stay in one place. I lean in toward the garbage and sniff. It doesn't smell like garbage. Well, it does smell crappy, but garbage has a particular kind of crappy smell. This just smells like someone sprayed some kind of crappy smell in the air to make people think there's garbage in here.

I wave my hand through the garbage. My hand passes right on through. It's a glamour.

North looks over at the two other men, and they all three grab onto the dumpster. I realize they're about to try to move it.

"Wait." I go up to the bricks on the wall right by the back lid of the dumpster, feeling along. Ah-ha!

I press on one and it sinks into the wall. I quickly step back, ushering the men out of the way, and the dumpster, along with the concrete that it's on and the wall behind it, all swing open slowly on a huge turntable. It reveals a huge, dark entryway. I can't see into it. My stomach twists.

North steps forward into the darkness. Well, I'm sure as hell not letting him go in there alone. And this is all about me and my problems, anyway. I step forward and follow him, the other two men at my back.

The dumpster and all the rest swivel back on us, closing with an ominous scraping sound, and for a second we're in pitch blackness.

Then a door opens, and light floods in as two men enter. They're both wearing suits and brass knuckles. I can't see anything, but I'm pretty sure that while we were stuck in the darkness, a security system checked us out to see if we're friends or had an appointment.

The two guards look us up and down. I can't quite

tell what kind of supernaturals they are. But they're not vampires, I know that much. Vampires are much paler than this and you can tell they have fangs because of how they hold their jaws. Their mouths just sit differently on their faces than supernaturals without fangs.

That surprises me a little. Donovan employs non-vampires? A lot of vampires are kind of elitist, they only want vampires in their groups, but I guess Donovan's more of an equal-opportunity sort of guy, as long as he's top dog.

"We've got something for Donovan," North says. Cain and Raven press up close to me, making it clear that they're protecting me. "We'd like an audience."

The two guards look at each other, then back at North, assessing. Probably wondering if they should throw us out on our asses and deal with this shit themselves, or if it's worth bothering the boss.

At last, one of them, the one on the right, nods. "This way."

I feel simultaneously relieved and more stressed. This is going to either clear my debt or go spectacularly wrong, and I have no idea which way it'll go.

We're led down a well-lit, narrow hallway, with doors on either side that seem to lead to offices. How boring and bureaucratic. I didn't see this part of things when I was last here. I came in through an upper window and made my way down to the area where the gem was kept on display. Personally, I think that if you have an Aurora Gem and you're showing it off in the middle of your damn evil villain lair you're fucking begging for it to be stolen by someone, but I doubt that telling that to Donovan's going to help. Criticizing how a guy was holding his gem when you stole it from him is not the way to get into someone's good graces.

I hope I don't have to tell Donovan anything at all. I hope I can just hand the key over, say sorry for stealing from him and that it won't happen again, and be done with it. I want out of here. I can sense the vampires and my skin feels like it's crawling.

The two guards lead us through a doorway, into a huge open area. It's almost like an arena. It's much larger than the outside of the building would suggest. Tall, vaulted ceiling stretch up high, like a massive cave that had the walls carefully smoothed over. Thin, Gothic columns hold everything in place. It kind of reminds me of a church, to be honest.

A few doors in the walls lead to other places. Just how big is this building?

This room was definitely built to impress. There's really no other reason for it. Donovan will never fill it with people. There will never be huge crowds that need to get in here. It's just to make anyone who walks in here feel small and know how much power he has, or wants to have.

It suggests a desire for power and an ambition that concerns me. I mean, I'm always concerned about vampires. They're ambitious assholes who want to destroy my kind, but this is a little more than usual. This isn't just simple arrogance. It suggests a lust for power that adds to my already close-to-frayed nerves.

Different people are milling about. I can see the vampires now, and my skin continues to crawl, a shiver working its way up my spine. I feel like a prey animal, and I hate it. Nobody ever gets the best of me. I'm not helpless. But fuck, I feel that way right now. I've literally walked into the lair of the bloodsuckers.

Raven puts his arm around me again, and I inhale carefully, exhaling slowly. I'm not alone, I remind myself. I've got three men with me, formidable fighters who've proven they'll do anything for me. They're here to support me. I don't have to do this alone.

I'm *glad* that I'm not alone.

Towards one end of the room is a raised area, with a large chair on it. Okay, to be honest it's a fucking throne. The arrogant dickbag has a damn throne in his fancy cave, like he's a king or something.

I honestly wonder if the new king of the North

American vampires knows about this sort of behavior. Vampires are really big into social standing and hierarchy. He probably wouldn't be pleased to find out that Donovan, technically the king's inferior, has set up a literal throne room for himself.

Maybe that's a tidbit to tuck away into the back of my mind and keep handy for later.

The man himself is sitting on his throne as the guards lead us up there. It's a big, dark wooden chair, with designs carved into it. The designed carvings have been filled with red, so that it now looks like the chair is covered in swirls of blood.

I shiver. I hate being afraid, but I can't help but remember my parents. What happened to them. What it felt like, how it looked. I take a few more deep breaths. Vampires can smell your blood and hear your heart beat. I don't want to give anyone in here the satisfaction of knowing that I'm nervous because my heart rate went up.

Donovan himself isn't how I'd pictured him. Not that I'd really pictured him at all. I'd expected someone a bit older in appearance, perhaps wearing a fancy pinstriped suit. Instead, before me is an insanely handsome man in his mid-thirties, wearing a vest and tight-fitting jeans. Like he's about to go out for a night on the town.

Of course, the mid-thirties part is misleading. Vampires don't age. Donovan's definitely been around for centuries if he's been able to amass this much power.

He lounges on his throne, a leg thrown over one of the arms, and he looks incredibly bored except for the sharp glint in his eyes.

"And what is this?" he asks as we approach. "I told you guys I prefer the trash taken outside."

"We're here as a peace offering," North says.

Donovan peers around North, his eyes settling on me. "Ah. Is this tasty morsel your offering?"

North swallows his growl. "She's the one making the offering."

Donovan looks confused, so I step forward next to North. "My name is Kiara, but you'll know me as the person who took your Aurora Gem."

"Ahhhhh. The little thief. The girl with the sticky fingers. Very unfortunate for you." Donovan smiles. "But I'm guessing that you're here to return my gem safe and sound?"

His voice is like velvet, soft, almost a purr, but there's something slimy about him that takes away all of his charm and handsomeness. I wouldn't want him anywhere near me if I could help it.

Unfortunately, I can't help it. I need to give him the key.

"No, I'm not here to give you the gem back. I gave it away to my client, and I don't have it anymore."

Donovan stands up with that terrifying speed all vampires have. "Then you are here to die?" he asks, his voice still soft and charming. It's alarming, the difference between his voice and his body language.

I force myself to stand tall. My parents wouldn't want me cowering in front of a vampire, or even a group of vampires, no matter how powerful they were. They didn't go down without a fight, they kept their dignity until the end, and so will I.

"Your gem was of great value," I explain. "And I didn't know who you were when I stole it for a client, or I never would've taken on the job. You have my utmost respect and deepest apologies."

Lies, but whatever. I can't get out of this by being flippant, even as my hatred for him and all vampires burns like the sun.

"I was unable to find a gem to replace yours, but I have something of equal or greater value that I'm sure you'll appreciate. Consider it an apology and a peace offering, so that we can go our separate ways and just... forget about each other." I stumble over my words a little at the end, but I think I did okay.

Behind me, I can feel all three men glaring. Donovan glances at them momentarily, but also dismissively. The other supernaturals in the room don't seem so inclined to ignore the men. Their reputations clearly proceed them, and the others are all eyeing them with a mixture of respect and apprehension.

It makes me feel a bit proud, actually. These three men are powerful and they've chosen me as their mate. It makes a girl proud.

And I'm really, truly glad that they're here and insisted on not letting me do this alone. I hadn't expected to feel so much fear churning up in my stomach.

"Well, what is it?" Donovan asks.

"I can't give you anything without a promise of my safety," I reply.

"And I can't possibly promise anything if I don't know what it is I'm being given," Donovan shoots back.

He walks down from the throne to stand in front of me. "What is it that's worth so much more than my precious gem? Your words are pretty but your apologies mean nothing. I want an item. Words don't mean anything without actions. Why shouldn't I make an example of you to every single lowlife who thinks for even a second that they can take me on or take what's mine?"

I take a deep breath. "Because I have an Immortal Key."

North hands it to me, and I hold it up for Donovan

to see. It's such an unremarkable key, a piece of cut-out metal that's a bit sharp around some of the edges, but the entire room reacts like I've just held up a massive grenade.

Donovan's eyes go wide and his fangs poke out, a sign of excitement in vampires. "Well, well, well. How very interesting. An Immortal Key, well, I haven't seen one of those in quite some time."

There are murmurs from the other supernaturals, everyone gathering around us to try to get a good look without crowding too close and pissing off Donovan or my men.

"Do you want it?" I hold the key a little out of reach. "You'll have to consider my debt to you paid."

Donovan seems to consider this for a moment. "Very well. If you give me this key, then your debt to me from robbing me of my gem is considered paid."

Good. That's all I want.

With a shaky breath, I hand the key over to him. Thank fuck. I can't believe this actually worked, and I'll have a mob boss off my back. It's like being able to breathe in fresh air after being locked inside a stuffy room for hours.

Donovan smiles eagerly as he snatches the key from my hand. His movement is rough, causing the sharp metal of one of the teeth on the key to catch against the palm of my hand, drawing a bit of blood.

"What—?" The vampire mob boss's eyes go wide. He grabs my wrist before I can even think to stop him, yanking it to him and licking up the bit of blood.

Disgusting. I yank my hand back as the men dart forward, Raven transforming, North snarling, the three of them pulling me to them protectively.

I cradle my hand to my chest. It wasn't a true bite, barely anything, but I still feel violated.

Donovan licks his lips, and as he does, his eyes go completely black. My stomach dips.

Oh, that's not good. That's really not good.

"Well, well, well," he purrs again, this time a full, proper purr, the soft silky voice of a predator. "I should have known, based on your smell. You're fae."

Everyone in the room reacts to this. The supernaturals all around us crowd closer, and I can see the vampires baring their fangs as various other creatures get battle spells ready.

Donovan won't really try to kill the men just to drink my blood, will he?

Hell, I shouldn't put it past him. We're in his lair, after all, and we're outnumbered ten to one.

"But not just any fae. Oh, no." Donovan clicks his tongue and shakes his head. "You're pure. Extremely pure. You have the blood of the ancient ones." He smiles, and it's the most chilling thing I've ever seen. "My master will have great use for you."

As if those words are some kind of secret signal to all of his fucking henchmen, everyone around us attacks en masse.

I whirl around to defend against a vampire who lunges for me, catching sight of Cain, North, and Raven throwing themselves into the fight too. The sounds of snarls, shouts, and grunts fill the space, but somehow, Donovan's deep laugh manages to rise up above it.

There's a good chance he'll lose people in this battle, even if they manage to overpower us in the end—but he doesn't seem to give a single fuck about that. I catch sight of him grinning as he watches the chaos before him, and then I have to yank my attention away, diving and rolling as my vampire attacker nearly gets a hold on me.

I start to phase out, but before I can, rough hands grab me from behind. Someone hits me with a spell so potent that it feels like I got punched in the chest, and all of a sudden, my body becomes fully solid. I try again to phase out, but I'm locked in corporeal form by whatever magic they just did.

On either side of me, I can see Donovan's lackeys swarming my three mates. They must've hit them with spells that keep them from transforming into their more deadly forms, just like they did to me to stop me from phasing.

My stomach drops all the way down to my feet.

Panic rips through me, and I redouble my efforts, fighting like I've been possessed. The men fight harder too, growling and snarling like animals.

But it's not enough.

An arm hooks around my neck from behind, cutting off my air as it squeezes tighter and tighter. I throw elbows and try to kick backward to take out my captor's knees, but he holds on tight, and my struggles get weaker as my vision darkens at the edges. Raven, North, and Cain have all been captured too, and for one heart-wrenching second, my gaze locks with Raven's, seeing the fury and fear burning in his eyes.

These three men are here because of me. They've been caught by a dangerous vampire crime lord because they accompanied me into his lair.

Damn it. I shouldn't have let them come. If Donovan kills any of them, I'll find a way to kill him.

That's the last thought I have before the world goes completely black.

ALSO BY SADIE MOSS

Magic Awakened
Kissed by Shadows (prequel novella)
Bound by Magic
Game of Lies
Consort of Rebels

The Vampires' Fae
Saved by Blood
Seduced by Blood
Ruined by Blood

The Last Shifter
Wolf Hunted

Wolf Called
Wolf Claimed
Wolf Freed

Academy of Unpredictable Magic
Spark
Trials
Thief
Threat
Hunt
Clash

Hidden World Academy
Magic Swap
Magic Chase
Magic Gambit

Her Soulkeepers
Sacrifice
Defiance
Ascension

Feathers and Fate
Dark Kings

Wicked Game

Wanted Angel

Claimed by Monsters

Bound to the Dark

Captive of the Dark

Queen of the Dark

Made in United States
Orlando, FL
28 January 2022

14100464R00171